SILENCED IN SALEM

A NINA BROWN PARANORMAL COZY MYSTERY

CAT GREEN

DEG PUBLISHING COMPANY

PREFACE

So excited for you to meet your *fun new friends!*

You'll find Jasper the star of the show.

He lives across from Central Park. Be certain to follow his adventures with his personal author newsletter.

CHAPTER 1

"Ghosts be all over Salem this Halloween weekend." The whiskered Amtrak conductor lowers his ruddy face to peer into my eyes. "Better keep your wits about you, young lady."

"I'm not afraid of ghosts." I smooth a wisp of hair from my forehead. It feels wilted after nearly four hours of train travel, just like my once-crisp white blouse.

"Then this must be your first trip to Salem. Plenty of ghosts here on this train, too. Tell me you don't see them?"

"I don't see them." My gold locket burns hot against my skin. *Never a good sign.* "And why would a ghost take a train? Wouldn't a ghost just *materialize?*"

"Depends on the ghost." The conductor snickers as he moves forward into the next cabin.

As the train rattles the last mile toward the Salem stop, I peruse the other passengers in my car. Most wear over-the-top costumes for the Halloween weekend. Sexy nurses. Werewolves.

"He's right, you know." The tattooed girl across from

me speaks through blue-painted lips. "Ghosts ride this train. And that one there? He's after you."

I turn. But I see nothing. No one.

As the train doors swoosh open at the Salem station, I feel someone, or *something*, following me. I quicken my step over hardened gum patches and cigarette butts, hurrying my way toward the exit.

Outside the MBTA station, I pull my coat tighter against the October chill. At barely 5pm, the sky's already indigo blue. A near full moon casts an eerie glow over waiting cars in the parking lot.

Two shrieking skeletons run by to my right. I gasp, then realize they're wearing light-reflective Halloween costumes.

Maybe coming to Salem, Massachusetts, on Halloween weekend wasn't such a good idea. *But Salem can't be any more dangerous than New York City…*

Or can it?

I scan the parking lot. The PR lady said a hotel car would be here to meet me.

"Miss Nina Brown?"

A darkly handsome man dressed as an 18th-century sea captain strides toward me in a deep blue velvet blazer over a white cotton shirt. The glistening pearl at his neck sets off the features of his finely chiseled face. He's attractive in a slightly older-man sort of way. Young enough to radiate vitality through his dark hair, defined black brows, and clear blue eyes. Yet old enough to command authority and inspire intimidation with his commanding demeanor.

"Yes, I'm Nina Brown." I arrange my long bangs over my forehead to better hide my raised scar. The best way to avoid the inevitable questions about its origin. "Are you from the PR agency?"

Based on his aristocratic deportment, he's certainly no lackey. But instead of answering or even introducing himself, the enigmatic sea captain nods. "I will escort you to your driver. Please, follow me."

He guides me toward a shiny black car at the curb. The gold insignia of the Salem Heritage House glistens on a card affixed to the window. Seeing us approach, the uniformed driver doffs his cap and opens the door.

The captain follows me inside to share the backseat. The air fills with his scent—cherry tobacco and spice.

"Tell me about yourself, Miss Brown," he says in an imperious tone.

I hesitate. If he came to meet me at the train station, why wouldn't he already know who I am?

"Well, you know I'm with *Travel! Food! Wine!* magazine. I work closely with Ruth Ross, the editor-in-chief."

I leave out that I'm her secretary, and that I set up this visit on my own, hoping to score my first magazine-feature byline. Even more important would win a big-ticket advertising contract for the magazine and getting a chunk of that commission.

The captain nods for me to continue.

"Last month, I received a press release announcing that the historic Salem Heritage House would open as a new luxury hotel. I wanted to be the first to cover it for the magazine. Now would you mind answering a few questions? Even with all my research, I couldn't quite determine what the Salem Heritage House had been before its transformation."

"It was a private home belonging to Captain James Hawkins," he says. "It stood empty for nearly two centuries."

"Empty? You mean closed to the public?"

He nods. "An express wish of Captain Hawkins. A custodian kept the house safe—a responsibility passed on to his descendants through the years."

"Kept safe from what?"

The sea captain looks off to his left, as if carefully choosing his words. "Captain Hawkins accumulated many valuable items during his travels. And there are rumors of hidden treasure."

"*Treasure?*" I read something about that in the press release, but I've grown numb to PR people and their sensationalist writing. One of my college marketing classes demanded we include a dramatic hook in every paragraph to keep readers engaged—even if we had to make it up. "Why is it opening as a hotel now?"

"Mr. Grant, the general manager, will tell you everything you need to know." The captain watches as I turn my attention to the view outside the window. "What do you think about Salem so far?"

"It's magical." Small shops line brightly lit streets. Snatches of antique-looking sailing ships on the wharf can be seen between old buildings. "My best friend, Holly, and I always dreamed of coming here. And now, here I am."

Within minutes, the car pulls up to the Salem Heritage House. Like the pictures I've seen in the hotel's press kit, it radiates a classic New England charm. Decorative brass adorns the large bay windows.

The driver opens my door, and I step out. But when I turn to say goodbye to the captain, he's gone.

"Wait." I turn to the driver. "Where's the captain?"

"Captain?" The driver looks up from the sidewalk where he's just deposited my rolling luggage.

"Yes. The man in the captain costume who was in the backseat with me."

Without answering, the driver nods a brisk goodbye, returns to his car, and drives off.

Odd.

Red and yellow leaves rustle in the wind as I wheel my suitcase toward the entrance.

A small, jet-black kitten meets me halfway, looking up with remarkably jeweled eyes. One's amethyst, the other jade green. When I pick it up, it rests its paws over my right shoulder and curves itself against my body.

"Hello, Ms. Brown," says a remarkably handsome man in a well-fitting suit. He has a subtle English accent and walks towards me with the elegance of that old movie actor from *Gone with the Wind*, Clark Gable. He sort of looks like him, too.

"Welcome to the Salem Heritage House. I'm Theodore Grant, the general manager. And I see you've met Pyewacket."

He gently pries the cat from my shoulder. "Now, Pyewacket…" he purrs in a voice as smooth as honey. "It's not ladylike for a little kitten to be so forward with hotel guests." He lowers her to the walkway and turns to me. "Allow me to carry your luggage inside."

"Thanks. Quick question—a man met me at the train station and escorted me to the car. He mentioned you by name. Who was he?"

"Mentioned *me*?" His voice reflects surprise.

"Yes. He was dressed as a sea captain. In Salem, I guess everyone gets into the Halloween spirit."

Something bright explodes in Mr. Grant's gunmetal gray eyes but fades just as quickly. "Perhaps he was from the Salem Tourism Council. They're aware of your visit as well. Come this way, please."

Dark shadows flicker against the hotel's white-framed exterior as we walk toward the entrance. Strange, since the sun has set by now. I breathe deeply, then step through the door.

CHAPTER 2

I follow Mr. Grant into what he had presented as the newest small luxury hotel in Salem during our phone call. But my shoulders slump in disappointment.

I had imagined a sleek, modern design. Instead, the classic New England-style décor of the foyer, with its crackling, wood-burning fireplace, resembles a scene from a dated Hallmark Christmas card.

The small living room reeks of stagnant air, an ambiance both gloomy and claustrophobic.

"Gorgeous." I force a smile.

"I'm glad you agree. Our team worked hard to fill it with as many of the original furnishings as we could find.

Do you see that tangerine-colored tapestry rug in the sitting area? Captain Hawkins, the original owner of the Salem Heritage House, brought it here from Persia. And this gorgeous crystal chandelier overhead? From Murano, Italy. You'll discover the Salem Heritage House glitters with priceless treasures."

Standing awkwardly, I reach for my notebook to write this down.

"Forgive me. You must be exhausted from your journey. Warm yourself here near the fire, and I'll bring you some hot tea while we chat."

Once he leaves the room, I rise to snap pictures to reference for my article. But this sad-looking dwelling is nothing at all like the quaint luxury inn I'd imagined in my mind's eye. *Should I stick out the weekend, or make up an emergency and go back home?*

Activity outside the large side window captures my attention. A man moves within an illuminated wire cage the size of a small room. *Odd.* After a moment, I realize he's in a foliage-filled aviary.

An enormous orange, yellow, and red parrot is perched on his arm. From my position, I glimpse his broad-shouldered back and sun-streaked blond hair.

When Mr. Grant returns, I take my place on the sofa, ready to take notes.

"We're a boutique hotel." Mr. Grant pours fragrant tea from an ornate, blue China pot edged in gold. "An *intimate* hotel for the privileged few.

We aim to give our guests an authentic Salem experience. Now, this weekend is what we call our 'soft opening'. When you and I began our conversation, I thought we'd be much further along in our renovation."

"Yes." I struggle to keep my tone upbeat, even though I'm furious with myself for not vetting the property properly. *Never believe a press release.* Hadn't my marketing professors hammered that into our heads? "Why the delay?"

Mr. Grant slicks back his tawny hair and flashes a charming smile. "The Salem Preservation Committee is quite strict. We're expecting our plans for additional expansion to be approved soon."

"But how soon?" I clench my fist to keep my voice

calm. "With all due respect, you led me to believe the hotel was completely refurbished and ready for guests. I blocked out the first six months of the new year for a series of feature advertorials in our magazine—"

"Have no worries," Mr. Grant says with a laugh, seeming to make light of my concern. "Everything will happen in due course. Now let me show you the architect's rendition."

I take a deep breath as Mr. Grant removes drawings from an expensive-looking leather portfolio.

He hands me a large, cardboard-backed drawing, enabling me to see the entire house at a glance. It's much smaller than I had expected. The ground floor comprises the living room where I now sit, a large dining room, a breakfast room, kitchen, and a small room to its side marked *service quarters*.

"As you see, guest bedrooms are all planned for the second floor. On our tour, I'll show you the ballroom on the third floor, featuring the original chandelier of Swarovski crystal. Tonight, as we discussed, I've arranged for you to interview the celebrity chef we've engaged to put our luxury hotel on the culinary map."

"I'm looking forward to that. But why the mystery? Why couldn't you reveal the chef's name earlier? Our readers are devoted foodies. We're expecting the cuisine here to play a large part in the feature article and advertorials—"

"You'll understand when you meet him. And the hotel's owner, Ernest Pinkley, is in residence this weekend from his home in Miami Beach. You'll meet him at our midnight séance tomorrow night, if not before."

"A séance on Halloween night?"

"Don't be afraid." Mr. Grant flashes a reassuring smile. "Fright tourism has always been a leading draw in

Salem—as are stories of witches, pirates, and buried treasure."

"I read something about a treasure in the press release. Can you tell me more?"

"Every pirate or sea captain worth his salt is rumored to have had one, including our own Captain Hawkins. Who knows, perhaps his ghost will reveal its location at the séance tomorrow. You're not superstitious, are you?"

I hesitate. "No."

"You're sure to enjoy it. And you'll find a surprise in your room to make you feel a little more comfortable."

"What kind of surprise?"

"If I told you, it wouldn't be much of a surprise now, would it?"

Rising, Mr. Grant moves to the highly polished wooden reception counter. He takes out a clipboard and hands it to me, along with an old-fashioned pen.

"Now, if you'll just sign the register for me."

My gut tells me to make an excuse and leave. The inn's eerie silence unnerves me. "Sign? I feel like I'm the only guest."

"Just protocol, my dear."

I sign my name with a flourish.

Mr. Grant takes the clipboard from my hands and places it in a locked cabinet. "We've put you in our best suite." After handing me a skeleton key, he gestures for me to follow. "You'll love the luxurious marble bathroom. The other renovations are pending approval."

A vision of a dusty, two-hundred-year-old broom closet pops into my mind.

As if reading my mental image, he laughs. "The room is beautiful. Quite pleasant. Freshly painted, bright, and airy. It boasts the original floorboards, giving it an old-world charm. We call it the Henrietta Suite."

"Who was Henrietta?"

"The daughter of Captain Hawkins' best friend. When Henrietta's parents died at sea, Captain Hawkins raised her as his own child, even though he was a bachelor. Come to think of it, you look a bit like her with that slender build and long, auburn hair of yours. Want to see her?"

"*See her?* Uh, what do you mean by that?"

"Come this way."

Mr. Grant leads me toward an elegant staircase. A red velvet carpet runner covers the center of the polished wooden stairs.

Mounted on the wall to the right is a near-life-sized oil portrait of a stunning girl. She looks about my age. The artist who painted her paid great attention to detailing her eyes. They shimmer with vivacity, as if she's alive, standing before me. I almost feel I should extend my hand to shake.

"Behold Henrietta." Mr. Grant speaks with affection, as if he's introducing a real person.

I rub the back of my neck to ease my growing tension. Comparison to a girl who lived in this house two centuries ago is creepy enough. *And now I'll sleep in her bedroom?*

"I don't think she looks like me at all." *Is it my imagination, or does Henrietta narrow her eyes at this remark?*

"Not exactly, no," Mr. Grant agrees. "But similar enough. You don't see that auburn hair color every day, not with those natural gold highlights—just like yours. And her eyes are that unusual green like yours, too. Sage green, I think they call it."

Mr. Grant studies me a moment longer. "How did you get that scar on your forehead?"

My fingertips reach to hide the raised z-shaped scar. "A childhood accident. A long time ago."

I glance at the portrait to Henrietta's right and freeze, my breath catching in my throat. "*Who is that?*" The man's a dead ringer for the captain who met me at the train station.

"Captain James Hawkins himself." Mr. Grant turns to look at me. "You've turned as white as a ghost. Why do you ask?"

I take a deep breath. "He looks familiar." I stop myself from saying more, lest Mr. Grant will think I'm as crazy as my mother. "Is there time for me to freshen up before the tour and meeting the chef?"

"Of course. Your suite's upstairs, the first on the right. You'll see a gold plaque with the name Henrietta Suite. Shall I help you with your bag?"

"No, I'm fine. I'll meet you in the foyer in a half hour."

I wait until he leaves before I mount the first step. But I feel someone staring at me.

Turning, I connect with the lifelike blue eyes in the portrait of Captain Hawkins. *He's staring at me.*

CHAPTER 3

At the top of the stairs, my black boots click along the hardwood floor as I walk down the hallway to the Henrietta Suite. Seeing the glimmer of a gold plaque, I stop in front of a tall wooden door. But someone's covered the plaque with a large, shiny gold cardboard star. *Jasper* is written on it with a black marker.

What is this? I insert the skeleton key into the lock and twist the knob to open the door.

"Surprise!"

A burst of light from a phone camera temporarily blinds me. As my eyes clear, relief engulfs me. My best friend and roommate, Holly Broad, pulls me into a hug.

"Holly, I told you I needed to come *alone* so I could focus on my job this weekend."

"Yeah, yeah, yeah. But I know you didn't mean it. So I took the early train. And guess who's happy to see you?"

Holly points to our pampered pooch, Jasper. Like a fashion model, our black and white French bulldog strikes a pose. He wears a black overcoat, wide white collar, and black hat with a shiny gold buckle—the costume of a well-dressed, 18th-century Salem Puritan dog.

Yipping happily, Jasper waddles toward me. When I pick him up for a cuddle, he plants a sloppy doggy kiss on my face.

Stepping into the room, I see that Holly's nearly recreated her office setup in the oversized living area of the Henrietta Suite. Tall ring lights illuminate her iPhone stand, designed for product photography. Her travel-sized sewing machine and a basket of fabric and trim rest on a table.

"What's all this?"

"While you're doing your reporter thing, I'll be photographing The Jasp for his new winter Uptown Dog fashion collection. Our Facebook followers have been asking for the new catalog. Come look."

Holly pulls me toward a corner of the room, where she's set up Jasper's doggy wardrobe. Tiny canine outfits hang from the steel bar of the portable clothing rack. A dozen dog-sized hats and scarves have their own lightweight plexiglass display.

"You could have just photographed him in Manhattan. It must have been a lot of work to lug it all here."

"The campaign is called New England in Winter. Jasper's Facebook followers demand the authentic touch. Besides, Jasper likes to feel the spirit of a place when he models the newest collection."

Leaping from my arms, Jasper pads toward the old-fashioned free-standing floor mirror. After admiring his reflection, he yips in approval.

"Look at that. The Jasp likes his outfit." Holly scoops our pampered pup into her arms. "Take a picture of us together so I can post it on Facebook. His fans love these impromptu moments. Here, use my phone."

Holly's her usual picture-perfect, Instagram-ready self. She wears her glossy black hair in a shoulder-length bob, the freshly applied blood red of her lipstick contrasting with her porcelain skin and jet-black eyes.

Today she's poured her hourglass figure into a white bustier and red polka dot skirt. A wide, black, patent leather belt shows off her narrow waist.

"I'm glad you and Jasper are here." I snap the picture and hand Holly her phone. "But, Holly, remember you're my guest. We're *both* guests of the hotel. Our behavior reflects on *Travel! Food! Wine!* magazine."

"Yeah, yeah, yeah—Oh! I almost forgot." Holly walks through a door leading to the bedroom and returns with a white bag. "I took a little stroll with Jasper to get the lay of the land. I found the cutest candy store and bought their Salem specialty for your mom, given her sweet tooth. How's she doing? Have you heard from the estate lawyer yet?"

I shake my head. "Julep sent me a video of the two of them making cookies this morning. Mom's fine. *Happy.* But I haven't heard anything from the lawyer yet.

That's why I absolutely must lock in an advertising contract by Monday. Winning this account would be a first-class ticket from penniless secretary hell to a lucrative position on the advertising team—so I could better support Mom. Now I need to freshen up before I go on a tour of this place and interview the chef."

"Ooh! That reminds me." Holly points at a table in the sitting room. "The chef sent up some Champagne and hors d'oeuvres."

I've been too preoccupied to notice the goodies arranged on the table. "Miniature lobster rolls." I snap a picture of the colorful display before taking a taste. "Delicious. The lobster is so fresh. And it tastes like it's infused with an herb." I take another bite. "Tarragon? Sorrel?"

"Who's the chef?" Holly pops open the Champagne and pours me a glass.

"They want to keep it a mystery until my visit. Apparently, he had three-star Michelin status at a previous restaurant."

"But *why* are they keeping it a mystery?"

"PR people like their surprises. But I'll find out soon enough. Did Mr. Grant tell you we're going to a séance tomorrow night?"

"Yes." Holly rubs her hands together. "Our first séance, in Salem. And on Halloween night too."

Popping the last of my lobster roll into my mouth, I move into the bedroom. With its twin canopy beds, Henrietta's suite does exude a luxurious charm. The fine silk bedspread feels fragile to my touch, as if thousands of silkworms spent their lives weaving its peaceful design.

"Isn't this gorgeous?" Holly plops herself on to her designated bed. "Like a fairy tale, right? I wonder what princess lived here."

"Henrietta. Captain Hawkins' ward. Mr. Grant showed me her portrait on the first-floor staircase. This was her room. Here's another portrait of her."

I walk toward the painting hanging above the nightstand between our beds. In this one, she appears more innocent, sparkling with the excitement of a life yet to come. Her white dress gives her a sweet, virginal look. In this portrait, she holds a black kitten, which looks a lot like the black cat who greeted me. *Pyewacket.*

"Beautiful." Holly crosses plump arms across her chest as she gazes at the long-dead girl. "It feels a little weird to be sleeping in her room—maybe even in her old bed. I wouldn't like anyone sleeping in my room after I'm dead."

"It feels weird to me, too. Look at the doll sitting on the dresser." I move toward the miniature version of Henrietta. "She's even wearing the dress from her portrait."

"Now that's spooky!" Holly says. Jasper comes over to see what we're talking about, and he barks at Henrietta's miniaturization.

"I'm going to take a quick shower," I say.

Holly nods. "I'll be in the sitting area, finishing up a brunch outfit for The Jasp."

I step into the large, mirrored marble bathroom and turn on the shower to ensure lots of hot water before disrobing. Steam's already rising as I step inside. The lavender body wash smells delicious as it slides along my skin like silk. Mr. Grant certainly didn't skimp on the amenities.

When I've finished, I open the door to change. Steam flows from the bath out into the bedroom, forming fluffy clouds around the room. Well, surely the wonky ventilation system's going to be among the things Mr. Grant fixes around this old place.

Then something in that cloud of steam *moves*. It stops right in front of the portrait of Henrietta.

"Holly." I raise my voice to be heard over the whirl of her sewing machine in the sitting room. "Come to the bedroom."

"For what?"

"Just come." When she enters, I turn to her. "Do you see what I see?"

"Steam. What about it?"

"That *face*. Do you see it? Eyes. The nose. *Her* mouth…"

"Did that glass of Champagne get to you or what?"

I watch as Henrietta's ghostly form takes shape in the

steam. Then it fades into her portrait. On the dresser, Henrietta's lookalike doll appears to be grinning.

"Forget it." It's been an odd day. *Maybe I just imagined it.*

Unzipping my suitcase, I dig around for jeans and a white T-shirt. Holly takes a snooping look through my stuff. "Good lord, Nina. What did you do? Raid the hairstyling section of the local Walmart?"

"I heard Salem's humid."

"Yeah, but no one needs that many tubes of anti-frizz, or more than one blow dryer for a two-day trip."

"The other one's an electric straightening comb. And what about you dragging around that sewing machine?"

"It's a miniature sewing machine, made for entrepreneurs on the go. I never know when inspiration will strike. Besides, you know Jasper likes to dress for every occasion."

"You're right about that." I quickly dress and grab my bag. "I'm going to tour this place, then meet the so-called celebrity chef. Be back soon."

As I step into the hallway, I wonder about Henrietta's formation inside the steam. My gut tells me it's only a matter of time before I see her again.

The crackling fire blazes brightly as I enter the foyer. Mr. Grant gestures for me to sit down.

"Ms. Brown, glad to see you looking so refreshed. Did you find Henrietta's suite to your satisfaction?

"It's lovely, thanks." I sink into the well-upholstered sofa and take my notebook from my bag. "May I ask a few questions before the tour?"

"Ask away."

"Tell me about Captain Hawkins. I understand this house was unoccupied for two centuries. *Why?* And why open it now? I didn't see that in any of the materials your PR person sent me."

"Because we're still not sure how to spin the story. What I will tell you is that after his death, Captain Hawkins mandated that the house be shuttered for two centuries, left to the care of the Salem Preservation Committee.

After that time, the house and his remaining fortune were to pass to his oldest living heir. That would be Ernest Pinkley III, now the owner of this establishment—or he will be tomorrow at midnight."

My fingers tighten on my pen. "This Mr. Pinkley, the heir. Did he grow up wealthy?"

"No. He was born here in Salem to a working-class family. But he had a knack for business and deal-making. In the last twenty years, he's purchased many of the properties on Essex Street and in the general vicinity. With his inheritance of the Salem Heritage House, he'll own what's referred to as the Golden Triangle of downtown Salem."

Mr. Grant sighs. "But as I said earlier, getting approval for the hotel's renovation is taking much longer than we expected. Let me show you the ballroom."

I follow Mr. Grant up two flights of stairs opposite the staircase I took to my room. He opens a door, revealing a large room with expansive windows and a polished hardwood floor. A majestic chandelier sparkles overhead.

"Behold one of the many treasures of the Salem Heritage House. This Swarovski crystal chandelier is priceless. It—"

Footsteps sound from the hallway. In a moment, a short, stubby man in a tan silk suit moves toward us. "Ah, Ms. Ross." A smile engulfs his fleshy face as he grasps my hand. "We're so pleased to receive an editor of your stature at the Salem Heritage House."

"A pleasure. But I'm not Ruth Ross. She's my boss and—"

Mr. Grant steps forward smoothly. "Ernest, allow me to introduce you to Nina Brown of *Travel! Food! Wine!* magazine. She read the press release and contacted me about featured placement in the magazine. I forwarded you the email earlier this week."

"Well, I didn't receive it." He looks me up and down. "What is your role at *Travel! Food! Wine!?*"

"I'm Ruth Ross's assistant."

"A secretary. They've sent a secretary to cover the opening weekend at my luxury hotel."

Out of the corner of my eye, I see a shadow. Something tiny and black climbs in through the window. It crawls along a decorative ledge around the perimeter of the room. In a single astonishing second, it leaps onto the chandelier. The chandelier crashes down, missing Mr. Pinkley by an inch.

Stunned, he looks at the fragments of priceless antique crystal rolling across the ballroom floor. "That chandelier almost killed me. And that cursed cat. I thought you drowned it long ago, Grant."

Ignoring his words about Pyewacket, Mr. Grant calmly taps his phone. "I'm calling the insurance company right now."

"Not a *word* of this in your article, young lady." Mr. Pinkley jabs a sausage-like finger into my face. "Not a word to anyone." He storms out of the room.

I look up at the ceiling for Pyewacket, but the cat is gone.

A tall, straight-backed man enters the room, his large ruby earring contrasting with his dark skin. He wears a luxurious gold brocade jacket, matching slacks, and a white shirt, giving him the air of an 18th-century butler.

"I heard the crash." He stops speaking when his eyes find the shattered chandelier. "What happened here?"

"As you see, the chandelier fell, almost killing Mr. Pinkley," says Mr. Grant. "Sweep the pieces into a container, as the insurance company will probably need them. Ms. Brown, would you mind finding your way to the kitchen to meet the chef? It's just through the dining-room door."

When Mr. Grant leaves the room, I realize the

costumed stranger must be an employee of the Salem Heritage House.

"I'll help." I get on my knees, moving the larger crystal fragments into a pile.

"Thank you kindly, miss. No need to trouble yourself."

He speaks with an accent I can't quite identify. Rising, I hold out my hand. "Hi. I'm Nina Brown. Nice to meet you."

"Moses B. Anthony." He seems surprised by my outstretched hand, uncertain what to do with it. "Did you see that chandelier fall?"

"It happened suddenly. Pyewacket leaped onto it. But I don't think she weighs enough to bring it down like that."

Moses' eyes flash as I describe what happened. But he says nothing more as he continues his sweeping.

Excusing myself, I leave to find the mystery chef. This visit hasn't started well. Hopefully, meeting the chef will make it right.

CHAPTER 5

I walk through the formal dining room toward the kitchen door. Opening it, I find the kitchen surprisingly modern, light, and airy. Sleek, white appliances gleam.

"Chef?" I call. "Chef? It's Nina Brown, the journalist here to meet you."

When no one responds, I open a door leading out to a large garden. I'm surprised to find the lavishly appointed aviary I first glimpsed through the window when I arrived. *Ultra-first-class accommodations for some lucky VIP bird.*

"Hello?" I venture closer to the aviary, attracted by the music emanating from it and its flashing tropical green, blue, and red lights. A mirrored disco ball spins in its center, and I recognize the song as the classic Barry Manilow tune "Copacabana."

Beneath the disco ball, the same broad-shouldered man lip-syncs along with the music. As he wiggles his shoulders and hips, the colorful parrot dances on a low table, bobbing its head and kicking out his legs. Every few seconds, it spreads its wings and squawks with pure enjoyment.

I speak loudly to be heard over the music. "Hello? Do you know where I can find the chef?"

The man spins around, allowing me to see his face for the first time.

"Brad?"

Chef Brad Collins? Fantasy of a million foodies. Star of more than a hundred culinary-focused TV episodes. Subject of hundreds of articles in glossy lifestyle magazines, each accompanied by his photo in crisp chef whites, his remarkable blue eyes seeming to gaze at the reader alone.

I was thirteen the first time I saw him smirking from the cover of my aunt's new issue of *Food & Wine* magazine. I still remember the thrill that rippled through my body. He was my first "older man" crush, though he'd only been a decade my senior.

I hadn't any idea I'd be working in his three-star Michelin restaurant, La Toque, a handful of years later.

His eyes widen. "Nina Brown? What are you doing here?"

Instinctively, I move to embrace him, inhaling his delicious scent—masculine, yet tinged with vanilla, like a fresh-baked meringue. "I could ask the same of you."

It's been over four years since we worked together at La Toque. Brad's kept his good looks, though he appears ragged around the edges.

"Welcome to my new life," he says in a slightly sardonic tone, hands outstretched to encompass the parrot, the corny music, and the colored lights.

Before I can ask what he means, the parrot flies to the tree branch between us, squawking in my face.

"Forgive me. I will make the proper introduction. Nina, this is Rico. Rico, meet my friend Nina Brown."

Rico squints one white-rimmed black eye at me, sailor style.

"I've never met a parrot before," I tell Brad. "Uh, hi. Polly want a cracker?"

"Don't be ridiculous," Rico croaks in an old man's voice. "*Parrots despise crackers.*"

Rico looks down his beak at me, then flies to a tree branch.

"Did you train him to say that?"

Brad shakes his head. "Not me. His former owner was a sailor. The two of them traveled the world for over half a century."

"How old is Rico?"

"The vet says seventy-five and still going strong. He's a crusty old fellow. But tell me about yourself, Nina. Grant told me a journalist was coming to interview me, but never in a million years did I imagine it would be you. What happened to that bright-eyed schoolgirl bussing tables between classes?"

"She's all grown up. And here to interview you for *Travel! Food! Wine!* magazine. Is there a place to sit so I can take notes?"

"Sure. I have a nice setup in the aviary. Rico likes my company, so I arranged for a desk and chairs inside his digs. Come in."

Brad pushes aside shiny, green banana leaves as he leads me into the room-sized bird cage.

"I never imagined you as a bird man."

"Me neither. But the local animal shelter had a booth at the Saturday market on Derby Street. Rico hit me up as I passed by."

"Hit you up? What do you mean?"

"He wolf-whistled at me. Then he said something like, 'Nice buns, toots.' I spun around and saw him. End of story."

"And the hotel built this aviary for him?"

"I did, actually. Rico demanded it. I'd originally planned an African forest setting in honor of his ancestors. But then I realized Rico had spent most of his life at sea with his late owner, so I gave it more of a nautical theme."

"But the colored lights? The disco ball? The music?"

"Garish, I know. And don't even ask me about the cost of his personal sound system," Brad jerks his head toward some high-tech-looking equipment. "But all the bird publications say parrots need constant stimulation."

I nod, faking a smile of understanding. It's hard to absorb how much Brad has changed from the slightly arrogant, confident celebrity chef he was when I worked at La Toque my freshman year at UCLA.

That was before the allegations of assault, which led to imprisonment.

Brad gestures for me to sit in one of two bamboo chairs with a low table between them. "Shall we start the interview?"

"Sure thing." I take out my black-and-white composition notebook and open to a fresh page.

Brad laughs. "Don't tell me you're still carrying around those old-school notebooks. I threw mine out in second grade."

"They're the tools of *my trade*, not yours." I point the tip of my four-color retractable pen at him, then click to black ink.

"Touché." As fast as a gunslinger in some old Western, Brad whips a chef's knife from a holster I hadn't noticed earlier. "I'm still using Chef David's famous knife, too. They don't make them like this anymore. Carry it everywhere."

"In case of a culinary emergency?" I ask with a smile. Then I remember Brad regarded the famous chef as the father he never had. "I'm sorry about Chef David's passing. I remember that day he came to visit the La Toque kitchen."

When Brad smiles, I add, "And speaking of kitchens, how is it that the kitchen here looks so sparkling new? The rest of this place looks like the stage set from that Addams Family TV show. All that's missing are the white sheets covering the furniture."

"Pinkley had the kitchen renovated before the Salem Preservation Committee clamped down. He built out the space for me—a little enticement to take the job, as if I had any actual choice."

"Job?" I lean toward him, my tone somber. "Tell me, how did all this come about? The last I heard, you were serving prison time for assault."

"I got my get-out-of-jail free card."

"I'm serious, Brad. Didn't you get something like five years?"

He sighs. "I'm in a special prison program—work while you serve time. Witch Wanda helped arrange it."

"Wanda?"

"Salem's local witch. She's running for mayor. Turns out she's a mutual friend of one of my buddies in Los Angeles. Wanda heard Ernest Pinkley was starting a small luxury hotel and needed a chef. She and my friends worked together to get me into the program. She was just here to drop off some fresh-baked brownies." He pushes a bright red tin box my way and uncovers it. "Want one?"

The brownies look good, but I shake my head. "You're working off your prison sentence here?"

Brad nods. "It was a bogus charge. Everyone knows it."

Bogus? Hard to say. The assault part was genuine. Brad admitted he fought his sous chef after catching him raping the restaurant's hostess in the wine cellar. But Brad didn't stop punching until he'd reduced the guy to a bloody pulp —a reaction, his defense attorney claimed, was born of the torture he'd experienced at the hands of enemy forces while serving with the US Army in Afghanistan.

The public had sympathy for Brad, especially since he'd been protecting a woman from a violent crime. Yet he was convicted, despite the post-traumatic stress syndrome defense his attorney put forth.

Brad had always impressed me as a fair but demanding boss. I witnessed no flares of temper or violent episodes. When the verdict of manslaughter came down, I was as surprised as every other culinary professional who knew him.

I touch his hand. "I'm glad you're in this program, here at the Salem Heritage House. And I'm happy you found Rico. You two seem good together."

At the mention of his name, Rico swoops down, landing on Brad's shoulder. The bird eyes me suspiciously. Then he knocks his beak against my shoulder.

"What was that for?" I rub my shoulder, more from surprise than any pain.

"Apologies, Nina. Rico's just *beaking* you."

"Beaking me? What does that mean?"

"It's a bird thing, specific to parrots. When they see a new object or human, they use their beak like a third arm to check it out. Rico, apologize to the nice lady."

Ignoring Brad, Rico leaps down to the table to pick a

walnut from a brownie. Then he nibbles from the
chocolate part of the brownie itself.

"So much for that," I say, wondering if Rico and I will
ever get to be friends. "Let's begin the interview."

Brad smiles and turns to me. Though he says nothing
with words, all he needs to say is in his eyes.

CHAPTER 6

"My first question is why the hotel was so secretive about revealing your identity before my visit."

"Off the record?"

"Sure." I put down my pen.

"Everyone's afraid of bad press. Pinkley and Grant thought it might put consumers off if they knew a convict was preparing their food."

"But they'll have to know *sometime*, right? I'm here to gather information for an article that will run when this place opens to the public."

"That time may be a long while off. A million things need to be done to make this so-called luxury hotel inhabitable."

"You got that right. Why did Mr. Grant and Mr. Pinkley want me to come so early?"

"I bet they wanted you to come Halloween weekend and attend the big séance tomorrow night. Fright tourism is a big thing here."

"Mr. Grant mentioned that."

29

"Spooky stuff that goes bump in the night brings bucks to the city. The Hawthorne Hotel down the street is famed for ghosts. It's booked years in advance for Halloween night. Grant's a sharp guy. Bet he figured if you knew the hotel was so far from opening, you wouldn't come."

"He's right. But I was counting on a fat advertising contract. I need to make real money, Brad. My mom… her condition's getting worse. So far, I've been able to keep her at home by employing a caretaker. But the estate lawyer wants to move her to an institution to save on expenses. I can't let that happen."

"Don't fret, Nina. It will work out. Life always has for you."

I try to let Brad's words bolster my confidence, but they're strange coming from him. "Back at the restaurant, you gave no one praise. What's changed you?"

"Rico. All the parrot-training books stress the importance of praising your parrot for small improvements."

Rico jumps to the floor of his aviary. He walks in unsteady circles like a drunk man. "Ghosts at the Hawthorne Hotel! Ghosts at the Hawthorne Hotel!"

"What's he doing now?"

"That Wanda." Brad shakes his head and sighs. "She must have put a little something in her brownies."

"Like marijuana? Isn't that dangerous for birds? And *people*, especially if they don't know it's been added to the mix?"

"It's not pot. Wanda doesn't do drugs. It's probably just an herb from her garden. Rico will be all right. At the very least, he'll sleep well tonight. Off to bed, Rico my man."

We watch Rico march off to the base of the nearest tree, slumping against it.

"If the hotel isn't anywhere near opening, what do you do all day? Kick back with Rico?"

"Oh, Pinkley keeps me busy all right. He wants me to flesh out the concept for this high-end French restaurant he plans to open after the first of the year. I'm planning the menu, but in my off-hours, I'm working on a cookbook."

"I'm not sure the world needs another celebrity chef cookbook."

"This one's different, Nina." Brad leans forward, his clear, blue eyes glittering in excitement. "Have you ever consumed pilgrim cuisine?"

"Like turkey and stuffing?"

"This is completely different. I'm calling it *Early American*. It has a ring to it, wouldn't you say? Grain-oriented food, lots of fresh herbs, and some seafood to round it out. What the pilgrims ate when they first landed at Plymouth Rock."

"What kind of herbs?"

"Indigenous herbs." Brad leans back in his seat, his jacket opening to reveal his tapered waist and close-fitting jeans.

"Indigenous herbs. Interesting. But can they be intoxicants? I read that's what could have created the witch-hunting frenzy."

"Even common herbs can have intoxicating properties. It depends on the part of the plant used."

"Is that what Wanda put in her brownie?"

"Could be. We exchange seeds, she and I." Brad stands. "Let me show you my garden. It's right outside the aviary."

Together we step into a beautiful herb garden the size of a paddle-tennis table. Mature trees stand guard behind a locked gate, shielding the plants from prying eyes.

"I had the idea of planting a garden like this while I was

in prison. I found this old book in the prison library about the natural herbs of Salem. It was a research project for some university kid in the 1970s, but some of his sources date back to 1605. That book told me everything I needed to know to make my garden grow. Old Moses helps me out."

"Moses?"

"The caretaker."

I remember the austere man who swept up the broken crystal from the chandelier. "Yes. I met him. Is it Mr. Pinkley who makes him wear that ridiculous servant outfit?"

"Pinkley thought it would add a historic touch for the dinner and séance tomorrow night."

"Moses seemed an odd sort."

"He's all right. He knows the herbs of the region well. His family's been here for generations."

"Generations?"

"Local Salem gossip says when Captain Hawkins sailed home from the east, his ship held an enormous treasure. Gold, according to the legend. Hawkins had a servant with him—a man he found in Jharkhand. And a parrot."

Brad laughs. "Possibly Rico's ancestor. Also sailing with him was Hawkins' good friend and the man's wife. But the treasure never made it to shore—and neither did his friend, or his friend's wife. Just their daughter Henrietta, Moses's ancestor, and Captain Hawkins."

"What happened to the treasure?"

"Captain Hawkins claimed it was lost at sea. Some say it can be found near Plymouth Rock. But most locals swear the treasure is buried in this house."

"So everyone who knew where the treasure might be buried is dead."

"Some say Henrietta knew the location and revealed it

in her diary. That diary's supposedly hidden in this house as well."

I laugh. "That's a colorful story to use in the advertorial I'm planning to write. That is, if the hotel ever gets permission to fully renovate and therefore needs to advertise." I look down at the herb garden. "What's this herb here?" I bend to touch a light green herb.

"That's araceae. The pilgrims called it sweet flag. If you eat the roots fresh, they're poisonous. But if you cook them, they thicken stews nicely. If you dry it, smoke it under a fire, then steep it in hot water like a tea. It's a great remedy for a headache."

I crinkle my nose. "It will either kill you or cure your headache?"

"That's the story for just about every herb growing here. And that's why I have a locked gate."

My smile wilts as I consider Brad's convict status. "You could be looking for trouble with this garden."

"No worries. In the right hands, the herbs are harmless enough. You won't believe the delicious taste of the labiatae plant." He kneels to break off a piece. "It's an aromatic herb that gives a special kick to salads. It's closely related to catnip."

As soon as Brad speaks the word, Pyewacket slinks toward us from the gate.

"Pyewacket. Get on over here."

The cat hurries over to him.

"Look at that, Nina. She smelled it from afar. Here, girl." Brad tears off a leaf and dangles it before the cat. "Gotcha a treat."

Sniffing it, Pyewacket rubs her furry head against the herb. Within a moment, she rolls in ecstasy all over the black dirt of the garden floor.

I point to another herb. "Is that parsley for your kitchen?"

"Looks like parsley, doesn't it? "The old puritans called it fool's parsley because it kills anything that ingests it."

"Why on earth do you have it? What if Pyewacket nibbles on it?"

"Most animals instinctively know when something they might eat can hurt them. Especially a cat like Pyewacket."

"But if people can't eat it, why do you grow it?"

"You never know when poison might come in handy," Brad says with a wink. "C'mon. Let me show you the rest of the place."

Brad scoops up Pyewacket and leads me back inside the house.

"Just a moment. Gotta give Pyewacket her sustenance." He opens the refrigerator door and measures thick cream into a beautiful, gold, antique-looking bowl for the purring feline.

"I never figured you for a cat man, either."

"Me neither. But we've formed a pact, she and I." As Brad bends to stroke the black kitten, Pyewacket brushes her body against his lowered hip.

Pyewacket seems to have him wrapped around her sleek, black tail. "Have you ever wondered if there's more to Pyewacket than she lets on?"

"What do you mean?" he asks.

I hesitate. "Mr. Pinkley was almost killed today. The chandelier fell just inches from where he stood. Since you were out here with the music blaring, you might not have heard it fall."

"What does Pyewacket have to do with it?"

"She was on top of the chandelier just before it fell." As I speak, Pyewacket stares me down with her amethyst and jade eyes.

Brad straightens to his full height. "Are you saying this cat tried to kill him?"

"No. She's just unusual, that's all."

I can feel the cat's eyes on me. She knows more than she's letting on. Much more. *But what can that be?*

CHAPTER 7

"As a special treat, I'm going to show you the secrets of the Salem Heritage House," Chef Brad announces. "Follow me."

He places his hand on my shoulder to guide me. His touch sends jolts of electricity through my body.

Pyewacket walks ahead of us, her black tail held high. She looks back, and I would almost swear she winks at me.

Brad leads me to a remote corner of the kitchen. In contrast to the shiny Subzero refrigerators and state-of-the-art appliances I first saw, this section looks as if it's not been touched in two hundred years.

"See this hearth?" Brad points to what looks like a fireplace against the rear wall. Above it, black iron hooks hold heavy copper pots. "This is how they used to cook food before the modern electrical oven."

Brad stands near the crumbling red brick wall of the original foundation. "Ready for some Nancy Drew action?"

"You bet."

"Watch this."

With little effort, Brad leans against the wall. A hidden door springs open.

"What's this?"

"A false wall.

"Where does it lead?"

"You'll see."

My pulse quickens as Brad guides me inside. When we worked together in the Los Angeles restaurant, we never touched—not even by accident in super-close restaurant quarters. Brad was always all business. Maybe that's why even his smallest touch sends spikes of pleasure through my body.

"Watch your step." Brad grasps my hand as we make our way up the uneven circular stairwell, its wooden steps sagging from moisture, neglect, and age.

The cracked beige walls bulge. To my right, a hairy black spider spins a web. Pyewacket hisses, and the spider darts away.

"How did you find this place?"

"The seven-year-old boy inside me found it. Secret passageways aren't hard to locate in old houses like these. Are you scared?"

"Should I be?"

Brad squeezes my hand. "A woman after my heart."

Two more spiders and a near-fall through the floorboards later, we arrive on the top floor. The last step creaks a dangerous warning as we reach the landing.

A splintered door rasps as Brad pushes it open.

Pyewacket snakes around us to enter first.

"This is Captain Hawkins' office."

I take in the ancient maps mounted on the walls and what appear to be logs of his voyages on the handsome wooden desk. Another portrait of Captain Hawkins is featured above the mantelpiece. In it, a parrot with Rico's coloring sits on his left shoulder.

"Hey, just like you said, he had a parrot too," I note with a smile.

Pyewacket looks up at the portrait, then stretches out on the luxurious red Persian carpet, seeming to enjoy the sensation of the firm wool on the soft pads of her paws.

"You are among the first to see Captain Hawkins' office in two hundred years—besides me and Pyewacket, of course.

"Mr. Pinkley must have seen it. Especially since it's his house now."

Brad shakes his head. "Not officially Pinkley's house. Not till midnight tomorrow. He has seen this study, though. You're right. He even moved himself into Captain Hawkins' bedroom just behind that door."

"What about Moses and Mr. Grant?" I ask. "They must have seen this study."

Brad's blue eyes gleam. "Of course. But as far as I know, you and I alone know of the secret passageway. I discovered it when Pye chased a mouse. I followed along, and voila."

Pyewacket hisses at Brad.

"Sorry. I meant *Pyewacket*." Brad turns to me. "She's sensitive about her name," he whispers. "Hates to be called *Pye*."

I walk along a wall of gold-framed portraits mounted against blood red, velvet-textured wallpaper.

"Henrietta, again." I stop. "This is the third portrait I've seen of her in this house."

"Beautiful girl. She looks like you."

"That's what Mr. Grant said. Frankly, I don't see the likeness."

Brad moves closer and gently turns me to face him. He

looks into my eyes. "I'm glad we have this chance to be together, Nina."

"What do you mean?"

"You didn't know? When we worked together at the restaurant, I always wished I had the freedom to ask you out for coffee or a drink. To get to know you better."

"Why didn't you?"

"Back then? That would have been robbing the cradle. And taking advantage of an employee. I was your boss. Now it's different. Or it can be."

Turning away, I stall for time. I want to accept. I want to respond with a kiss and embrace like girls do in romantic movies before the ending credits. But I remind myself I'm here as a professional. I can't make the situation worse than it is now.

"What's this?" I look at a small square door built into the wall with a handle.

"A dumbwaiter. All the old houses had them to transport food from the kitchen. See?" Brad turns the handle to open it. In it sits a large, boxlike wooden frame suspended in a shaft. "People would use pulleys to tug it up and down floors."

"What's over here?" I move toward the French doors on the far side of Captain Hawkins' study.

"It's called a widow's walk."

"Did Captain Hawkins even have a widow? Where would I see her portrait?"

"From what we know, Captain Hawkins never married."

"Then how can Mr. Pinkley be his heir?"

"A distant relation, I hear. But let me show you the widow's walk." Brad opens the doors to the night sky. "Some prefer to call it a roof walk. You'll find these low, rectangular platforms in almost every Salem home.

Women wanted to be the first to see their husband's ship sail in from foreign lands."

Brad flings open the doors. The chill air sweeps over me as I inhale the salty sea breeze from the Atlantic.

I step back quickly.

"What's wrong?" he asks.

"Oh, just my usual case of acrophobia." I keep my tone light.

"Fear of heights?"

I feel myself sway, though I'm wearing flats and standing on firm ground. "When I see a sharp drop like that, I get dizzy and imagine I'm falling."

Brad shakes his head. "But we're a full six feet away from the latticed iron wall. You'd have to be a world-class jumper to reach the edge."

"I know." My heart beats wildly, like some crazy drummer. I step back. "It's just a freak thing. I'd rather not talk about it."

Shrugging, Brad closes the doors and leads me away.

Back in the safety of the interior room, I look around and notice the primitive animal scent of ancient leather. I search out the source: Captain Hawkins' wall of books. I walk over to examine the ancient volumes, so many leather spines with gold lettering. "Now this is a treasure to me." I run my fingers across the books' fragile, cracked spines.

Brad laughs. "Nina *Bookworm* Brown. That's another thing about you the years haven't changed."

I spin to face him. "What do you mean?"

"Your nickname at the restaurant. *Bookworm*."

"I never heard that."

"Maybe you didn't want to hear it. You were always trying so hard to fit in."

A dim memory of my freshman year flashes through my mind. I was among the youngest on the restaurant staff and the sole female combination of busser and runner. This meant I cleared dirty plates from the tables and ran back and forth to the kitchen to get things.

"The staff called me a bookworm? Why?"

"They knew you were going to UCLA. On your off days, you said you were 'studying.'"

"You're right about that. Not sure all that studying paid off. Financially, anyway." I focus my attention on the old books before me. "Have you read any of these?"

"Reading isn't my thing. I prefer to live life in the raw."

"That will be your epitaph, like Alexander The Great. Brad Collins: Living life to the Max."

"You got it. Strike it big or go home, I always say."

I smile, but a sense of sadness overwhelms me. Brad always went for the gold. *How did he end up a convict, working out his prison sentence in an unfinished Salem hotel?* "What if one of these old books reveals where the treasure is found?" I ask, trying to keep the mood light.

Brad smiles as he approaches. His long fingers reach out to twirl a lock of my hair. "Does your imagination always work overtime like this?"

He bends down as if to kiss me, but his watch dings. "Shoot." Brad grimaces as he pushes a button to shut off the sound. "I have a call with a potential restaurant investor. We must leave."

"Wait. While we're here, can you show me the bedroom?"

Brad's eyes light up in surprise.

"That didn't come out right." I laugh. "I mean, will you show me Captain Hawkins' bedroom? That's where he was killed, right?"

Nodding, Brad walks over to the French doors. He pulls at the handles. "It's locked. Let's go the other way."

He leads me toward what looks to be another section

of books. He stamps his foot once, and the wall cracks open half an inch.

"What is this?"

"Another hidden passageway."

"How did you find it?"

"Research, Bookworm. Research." He winks and pushes the door open.

When he closes it behind us, I inhale a thick cloud of dust, the dust of centuries. As I step forward, my hair catches in a lacy spider web. My stomach turns as I find flies in it, and I quickly finger-comb the web out of my hair. "Where are we going?"

"You wanted to see Captain Hawkins' bedroom, didn't you?"

"How many secret doors and passageways does this place have, anyway?"

"Many."

We enter another vestibule, this one containing crumbling, red-brick risers and what look to be circular cut-outs in the thick wall.

"What the…?"

Brad puts his finger to his lips. "Stand on that riser." He gestures toward the taller one.

I step up and peer through the cut-out in the wall. My jaw drops as I gaze at a stunning, lavishly decorated bedroom. Everything in it is blood red, even the fabric-covered walls.

"Why is there a secret passageway linking his bedroom and office? Then another one up from the kitchen?"

Brad shakes his head. "I've thought about that. Maybe he wanted an escape plan if intruders stormed the house. Eventually, thugs stormed the house and killed him. So, the secret passageway didn't quite work."

A few moments later, Brad takes me back to the kitchen, the same way we came up.

When we reach the ground floor, he turns to me. "It's good to see you, Nina. It's been too long."

Before we part ways, I realize we didn't finish our interview. Well, we have the entire weekend ahead of us. There will be time.

As I leave the kitchen, I make my way past the dining room. Before I go up the stairs to my suite, I pause at the portrait of Henrietta.

Is it my imagination, or do her eyes gleam?

Just you wait, she seems to say. *Just you wait.*

*a*s I open the door of the Henrietta Suite, the gentle whirl of Holly's portable sewing machine vibrates in the air. "Hey, guys, I'm back."

When Jasper waddles over, I cuddle him. "Holly, I've just met the mysterious celebrity chef."

"And?" She turns to look at me. "Who is it?"

"Brad Collins."

Her jaw drops open. "What's he doing here?"

I quickly explain.

Turning off her machine, Holly stands, putting her hands on her hips. "Did he seem happy to see you?"

"More than happy. He didn't come out and say it, but I sense he had a crush on me when we worked together. Back then, I was young. *And* he was my boss. Now we'll just wait and see we'll see what the future holds."

A slow smile crosses Holly's face. "I've seen that light in your eyes before, Nina. That's your I'm-*falling-in-love* look."

"I'm not falling in love. I'm just glad to see him after all these years." I change the subject. "What shall we do for dinner?"

"We're meeting a friend of mine." Holly grabs her jacket.

"I didn't know you had a friend in Salem."

Holly's eyes gleam. "He's a new friend. I met him on the Internet."

"A dating site?"

"No. He runs the Facebook group for the Salem Tourism Council. I was trying to find good places to go, and we ended up getting friendly. We're meeting him at Flying Saucer Pizza. It's supposed to be one of the cooler haunts around in the area."

Holly wraps a warm cape around Jasper, still dressed in his pilgrim outfit. She tosses me my coat. Then the three of us head out into the night.

Eight PM seems to be the universal dinner hour around the world. Despite the cold, the streets of modern Salem blaze bright with the neon lights of violet-hued psychic shops and restaurants—almost like a mini Las Vegas.

Salem's chilly air refreshes me as we walk down bustling Essex Street. The tantalizing aroma of roasting chestnuts wafts from every street corner, stimulating my appetite.

We jostle past goblins, demons, witches, and skeletons, all part of the weekend's Halloween fun. Or maybe they're the real thing. After all, *this is Salem.*

On my right, I read a colorful advertisement for a "witch bottle" exhibit at the Peabody Essex Museum, one of the oldest, most prestigious history museums in America.

"Hey, look at that," says Holly, pointing at the sign with one hand as she jiggles a bundled up Jasper with the other. "I've never heard of a witch bottle. Do we have time to visit a museum this weekend?"

"We'll see," I say as we continue through the crowded streets.

Shops advertising fortune telling and tarot card reading appear at every turn. But then we pass by one more lavishly designed than the rest. Towering above a large video screen is the figure of an attractive woman with black hair, except for a pronounced streak of white streaming from her left temple.

She wears a purple dress and has an athame—a ceremonial witch's knife with a black handle—in a holster slung low around her hips. The screen below her plays video of her performing a slick illusion with smoke and mirrors. Two large guards flank the entrance to her shop, and there's a long line of customers in front of it.

"That must be Witch Wanda," I say.

"You know her?" Holly looks at me with surprise.

I shrug. "Brad mentioned her today. She helped him get his gig at the Salem Heritage House."

"Would you like to have a reading?"

"No. Let's go, or we'll be late to meet your friend."

"Surprise! I asked Noah to use his influence to book a reading for you."

"Why would you do that?"

"It's Halloween weekend, for one. Second, you're writing about Salem, right? You'll need to throw in a visit to a clairvoyant, or what's the point? And third…"

"Yes?" I cross my arms over my chest. "What's third?"

Holly sighs and takes both my hands in hers. "Maybe it's time you revisited that gift of yours."

"What are you talking about?"

She raises one eyebrow. "The moment earlier this evening when you asked me if I saw Henrietta's ghost in our room."

"You said you didn't."

"Right. *I* didn't. And I was too caught up in my sewing to give much thought to what you said—*at the time.* But then I realized that now that you're in Salem, your powers might be returning."

"Powers? You make it sound like I'm some sort of comic superhero."

"Well, gift then. Whatever you want to call it. Your sixth sense, as it were."

"And what if it was? It's not like I'm going to hire myself out to perform party tricks. Or set up a psychic shop."

"Just go in and have a reading. I'm curious what it might be like."

"If you're so curious, go yourself."

"We're here for your story. You're the writer, not me." Taking me by the hand, Holly drags me over to one of the tall, solidly built men guarding the entrance and gives him my name. After consulting his clipboard, he opens the red velvet rope. Holly charges forward to join me.

"Sorry, miss. Clients must enter alone," the man tells her.

"Rude, rude, rude!" Holly shakes her head. "Well, go on in, Nina. And you have to tell me all about it!"

After a moment of hesitation, I enter the almost black interior. Beneath a violet spotlight, the witch sits alone with a deck of tarot cards and several crystal balls before her. Dramatic lighting casts eerie, black shadows, exaggerating Witch Wanda's shapely form on the purple wall behind her. The sharp spice of patchouli oil burns my nostrils.

Witch Wanda's black tresses, with that streak of white, gleam as they cascade down her shoulders. The silver design on the black hilt of her athame shines under the overhead light.

"Hi. I'm Nina Brown."

Witch Wanda turns toward me, studying me in the detailed, careful way an art expert might examine a painting for forgery.

Rising, she glides the three steps from her dais to my level. She brushes away my bangs, exposing the scar on my forehead. "How did you get that scar?"

My hand rises to my left temple. "My appearance is none of your business."

"I wasn't asking about your appearance. I was asking about your scar." She hovers the open palm of her right hand just above it. Then she yanks her hand away, as if burned.

"A man named Noah made an appointment for me."

Witch Wanda gestures for me to sit down. "It's rare that colleagues book a visit."

"Colleagues?"

"Fellow clairvoyants. Usually, they just scry the future for themselves."

"Scry?"

"Typically, with a magic mirror." Witch Wanda peers at me more closely. "Can it be you are unaware of your gift?"

How can she know this? I decide to play innocent. "Gift? What does that mean?"

"Come sit at my table." She leads me up to her dais, then gestures for me to sit down. Besides the tarot cards, the table holds crystal balls in varying sizes and colors.

"Let me see your palms."

I open my right palm to her. She looks at it casually, using her forefinger to trace one line. Then she laughs loudly.

"What did you see?"

"The time you dressed your dog as a pirate for Halloween."

"Aren't you supposed to tell me *serious* things about my life?"

"Like what?" she asks.

I think about typical things a customer might ask a psychic. "Like how long I'll live? If I'll get married? How many kids I'll have?"

Wanda looks at me, arching one brow above her heavily made-up eye. "I don't want to bore you with the typical tourist trash. How about I tell you about the time you saved your friend's life when you were eight years old?"

"How did you know that?"

Wanda sits back and looks at me. "It's written all over your aura. I see you leading the cops to the car where that creep abducted her. You're still clinging to that memory. Why?"

For a moment, I'm too surprised to speak. "It's not that I'm clinging to it. Holly and I are best friends. We're always together. That's our bond. But I thought you were supposed to tell me the future."

"Some people have the future written all over them. Other people carry the past like a badge of honor. I call it like I see it."

"I'm always thinking about the future."

"No, you're not. You're stuck in the past. I see an older man saying you need to look to the future. He's lecturing you. Not your dad, but like your dad."

"Uncle Snicker," I say without thinking. "When I was a kid, he was always telling me to focus on the future, be prepared, stuff like that."

"I see a woman. Attractive. Sitting in an executive chair with silk-stockinged feet propped up on her desk. Manolo Blahnik shoes—the expensive ones with those red soles."

"Ruth Ross." *Of course, my boss inserts herself into my*

reading. I peer toward Wanda's crystal ball to see the activity within. "What's Ruth doing now?"

Witch Wanda doesn't answer right away. "Instead of seeking guidance in a reading," she says, standing. "I suggest you take responsibility for yourself. You're not eight years old anymore. Holly may not always be around to beat up the baddies, so they stop teasing you on the playground."

"What?" I just sit there, ashamed, and shocked at how this witch woman can see so far back into my schoolyard past.

When I don't move, an assistant I hadn't noticed in the back of the room approaches. She lightly helps me up and walks me out of Witch Wanda's lair.

Next thing I know, I'm back on the sidewalk.

"That was short!" Holly rushes to catch up with me as I exit. "Did she say you'll meet a handsome prince and live happily ever after?" From Holly's arms, Jasper taps my shoulder with his paw, as if he, too, is eager to hear the details.

"Private conversation!" I make a zipping motion in front of my lips. "Let's just go meet this Noah guy of yours."

Holly's mouth pops open, but when she sees my expression, she nods. "Okay. Fine."

As we walk toward Flying Saucer Pizza, a pang of fear stabs my stomach. Witch Wanda discovered my secret. *Now, what to do about that?*

CHAPTER 9

Flying Saucer Pizza is a boisterous, casual, sci-fi-funky place its name well describes. With Halloween just hours away, nearly everyone's dressed in costume—vampires, Frankenstein monsters, sexy nurses, the whole gamut. They sit at the tables eating pizza and laughing together.

"Which one is Noah? Ghoul or goblin?" I joke, surveying the crowd.

Before Holly can answer, a friendly looking, dark-haired man around our age walks up to her. "Holly?"

"Noah? How did you know it was us?"

"This little guy over here." Noah gently pulls Jasper from Holly's arms. "That picture of him in his pilgrim outfit was a hit on our Facebook page."

Noah rocks Jasper in the crock of his arm, tickling his soft pink tummy. The Jasp closes his eyes, emitting a little growly growl of pleasure.

"Noah, I'd like you to meet my best friend and roommate, Nina Brown."

Noah flashes a welcoming smile. "Ladies, and Mr. Jasper, I have a table in the back. Let me take you over."

As we find our seats, I look around the restaurant. One wall features a colorful 1950s-era view of outer space.

A server arrives immediately, asking Noah if he'd like the usual. He nods and asks us our preferences as he places the order. I study him as he chats with her. He's good looking in a best-friend-of-the-leading-man kind of way—medium height and dark, toffee brown hair, with a cowlick like a ten-year-old boy.

He's a little soft around the belly, with creamy skin and soulful brown eyes the color of a milk chocolate M&M.

Once the server leaves the table, Noah turns to Holly. "Tell me about your life in the Big Apple."

"It's very exciting. I'm doing a great business custom-designing doggy duds. And you can see Jasper loves being the brand ambassador."

Jasper yips his agreement from Holly's lap.

"But my real passion is designing BBW ensembles."

"What's BBW?"

"Big, beautiful women. Curvy girl fashion. *Like moi.*" Holly shimmies her shoulders. "I tried to get investor seed money. That was tough going. That's why I changed to doggy fashion."

Noah turns to me. "Holly told me you're doing a story at the Salem Heritage House for *Travel! Food! Wine!* magazine."

"Yes. And to be honest, I'm a little frustrated. I was led to believe it was a luxury hotel just about open for business. But the core renovations haven't even begun."

Noah nods. "Mr. Pinkley ran into some trouble with the preservation committee. They can be strict."

"When will it be resolved?"

He shrugs. "Your guess is as good as mine. But until it is, old Pinkley's doing his best to get them on his side."

"Bribery?"

Noah shakes his head. "No evidence of that—not that I've heard, at any rate. But tomorrow night, he invited me and some folks from the preservation committee to dinner and a séance. Probably because he wants to sway us to his cause."

When the pizza arrives, the aroma of fresh basil wafts toward my nose. Noah uses the cutter to divide the pizza into triangles.

After that, neither Noah nor Holly bother to use utensils. They grab their slices, giggling like a pair of kids. Gooey cheese oozes off the sides as they angle it toward their mouths.

Their gusto at the pizza, and each other, pleases me. It's good to see Holly with a nice guy for once.

When we finish, Holly requests dessert.

Noah smiles at her. "Great idea. What would you ladies like?"

"Anything chocolate for me," says Holly. "But vanilla for The Jasp."

I raise my hand. "Strawberry for me."

"How about the Witchy Neapolitan?" he suggests. "Vanilla, strawberry, and chocolate all together inside a witch's cauldron made from dark chocolate."

"Perfect, Noah." Holly looks around the room. "This is a fun place. From the way people table-hop, it seems everyone knows each other."

"Yep. It's a neighborhood hangout, all right."

"Who's that girl with the sparkly red shoes?" Holly touches Noah's arm. "She looks like *Sabrina the Teenage Witch* from TV."

I check out the teenager's costume, a sequined bodice,

ballet-like skirt, and a sparkly magic wand—perfect outfit for a five-year-old's magical playdate. "She looks more like Glinda the Good Witch from the *Wizard of Oz* than Sabrina."

Noah grins. "That's Blair Blanning. I went to high school with her big sister Becca. Their family owns a vintage dress shop off Derby Street."

A blast of cold air hits the room as the restaurant's front door opens. Witch Wanda enters, looking the epitome of a dark princess in her flowing purple gown, gold jewelry, and athame at her waist. Two bodyguards trail behind her.

Nearly everyone in the restaurant turns to watch her enter, including Blair Blanning, the teen witch. Blair hisses in Wanda's wake. Then she shakes her pink plastic wand at the famous witch's backside with such violence that glitter showers down on her pizza.

If Wanda noticed Blair's overt animosity, she doesn't show it. Once seated, Wanda speaks briefly to a server and turns her attention to her phone.

Just what kind of witch is Wanda? Based on my interaction with her, she has natural clairvoyance. Brad holds her in high esteem. But I sense there's something more to her. Just what it is, I don't know yet. I have the entire weekend to find out.

CHAPTER 10

The Neapolitan ice cream in a dark chocolate cauldron arrives with great fanfare and more than a few envious looks from diners around the room.

We dig in. Noah even asks for an extra spoon so he can feed Jasper some of the vanilla part.

"You like dogs." Holly's voice rings with approval. "Not every guy does."

"I've wanted a dog since I was a kid. But we weren't allowed to have one where I lived."

I take a bite of the strawberry section as I look at Noah. "Are you from Salem?"

"I was born here, but my mom and I moved to Boston when I was thirteen. I came back after college and have been here ever since."

"Why did your family move?" Holly asks.

Noah hesitates. He lowers his eyes to focus his attention on stirring his coffee. "My dad lost our family store in a gambling debt."

"That's terrible." Holly puts her hand on his. "I've read

about that kind of thing in novels. I've seen it in old movies, too. What type of store was it?"

"A candy store on Derby Street."

"Rotten luck. You must have made a fortune from the tourist trade."

Noah shrugs. "When I was a kid, there weren't as many tourists as there are today. But the store provided our family with a comfortable income. Best of all, it made me a big shot with the kids from my school. They'd all visit after class, and my grandpa would give them treats."

"Your grandpa worked there. Nice," says Holly. "I never knew my grandparents."

"It was a family store." Noah's eyes shine. "Owned since the 1800s. We specialized in old-fashioned candies like Sweetie, Top of the Mornin', and—"

"Top of the Mornin.' What a weird name for a candy." Holly laughs.

"It's a family specialty. It's made from sugar, mostly, like rock candy. But the story behind it made it famous."

"What's the story?" I lean forward, really liking Noah. *And liking that Holly likes him, too.*

Noah licks the ice cream from his spoon. "My ancestors arrived from Ireland on a boat with all their possessions. But before they reached Salem, pirates overtook the ship. They forced everyone off the boat and sailed away with their valuables. Somehow, my ancestors made it to Salem alive."

"How?"

Holly's fully engrossed in his story. Even Jasper leans forward, his front two paws on the table.

"I guess they swam to shore, from what I've read in the old documents. But they had nothing—no money, no relations, nowhere to live. When the local people found out my ancestor had been a candy maker, they gave her a pail of sugar. She used it to make Top of the Mornin' rock candy. People bought it, and it became so famous my family earned enough money to buy a store."

"It must have devastated your mom to lose the family shop." I touch Noah's hand. "Not just because of the money it brought in. It was her family history. Yours too."

"Yes. But she was strong." Noah digs for his wallet and opens it to reveal a picture of his mom. He keeps it where most people have their driver's license. She has kind eyes, a lot like Noah's.

"She acted fast. She didn't have money or family members to rely on, and then my dad flaked out, so she moved us to Boston. She worked hard to support us. Her dream was to send me to college. I did the best I could to get good grades and win a scholarship, and I graduated from the University of Massachusetts. Got my diploma on my wall."

"Good for you," I say.

Noah nods. "I always dreamed of making enough money to move Mom back to Salem and buy back the candy store, but..."

Noah stops mid-sentence.

"But what?" I ask.

"I've been back in Salem for two years now, and I haven't made enough money for either. And the man who grabbed the candy store in that card game refuses to sell."

The sadness in his voice is palpable. Holly and I look at one another for a moment, while Noah collects himself.

"How did you end up in tourism?" I ask, turning to a brighter subject.

"I fell into it," he says. "I've always had a passion for Salem, so I moved back here after college. I got a dead-end job selling ice cream at an Essex Street shop. That's where I met Wanda."

"Witch Wanda?"

Noah nods. "She must have heard me telling ice-cream buying tourists about Salem's amazing history and all the off-the-beaten-path places they should try. She told the head of the Salem Tourism Council they should hire me, and they did."

"What a well-connected witch." I regret my snarky tone as soon as I say these words. "I didn't mean for it to come out that way, Noah. I'm grateful for you arranging the meeting."

"You didn't enjoy your session with her?"

"She told me a little more than I wanted to know."

Noah nods. "Wanda has that reputation. I've found most Salem witches are on the up and up. Mostly, anyway. Tourists come here thinking Essex Street witches are just in it for the money. But most of them are real pillars of the community. Take Wanda. She was born here and has been practicing Wicca since she was a high school kid. I hope she's voted in as our next mayor."

"What's her platform?"

"Moderation. I know that sounds crazy—a moderate witch. But she grew up poor, like most of us. Tourism brings jobs to the city. Feeds our local families. She knows we need to attract the tourists yet keep a firm rein on overdevelopment."

Holly scoops up the remaining ice cream. "Translate, please. I don't know what you're talking about."

"Salem's broke," Noah says. "Some local politicians think the way to go is raze the old buildings and create a shiny, new Disneyland version of Salem's history. Wanda's *very active* on the Salem Preservation Committee. She thinks there's a way to protect our historical monuments and low-rise buildings, and still encourage tourism. Fright tourism drives our economy."

Noah grows more passionate by the moment. "It's what our agency considers the real reason people visit Salem—or Transylvania. They've read the stories like *Dracula* or read about the Salem witch trials in fourth grade. Now they want to see it in person. But many of them want the shiny, sugar-coated, amusement-park version. Wanda is against this type of development, and frankly, so am I."

Noah's red in the face by the time he stops talking, a little out of breath, too. "Sorry I climbed on my soapbox," he says. "I get carried away when I think of the small-town Salem I grew up in."

"Back then, we had other industries to support families. But they've moved on, leaving almost everyone in Salem completely dependent on the tourists. Without them, every hotel would be empty. Unemployment would be through the roof. Families couldn't afford to put bread on the table. That's where the Salem Tourism Council comes in. And that's why I'm so thankful to be running their social media channels."

"You say Wanda grew up here, poor. But the way she looks and acts, anyone would take her for a Las Vegas diva," I say.

Noah laughs. "She spent a few years out in Sin City, star struck by all those sequins."

"Did she tell fortunes?

"No. She did stage magic. Worked with an illusionist. Then she took his secrets and set up her shop."

"But she doesn't do stage magic here, in Salem, does she?" I ask.

"She doesn't call it stage magic," Noah says. "But I can see her stint in Vegas influenced the way she conducts her séances. The tourists love her theatrical approach."

Holly raises her hand. "Speaking of tourism, I have a question."

"Go for it."

"Like most tourists, I want to see where the witch trials took place. But do you think the witches hung or burned during the trials resent tourists trampling all over their graves?"

Noah is quiet for a moment. "I'm not sure how they feel about it. But I figure if there is such a thing as an afterlife, these witches would want to be remembered, even if it means tourists stepping on their graves."

Holly nods solemnly. Then she brightens. "Noah, we must fit Salem into a single weekend. Do you have time to show us all the fun, witchy things to do?"

Before he can answer, the teen witch approaches our table. She giggles as she taps Noah on the shoulder with her plastic magic wand.

"Noah! Why didn't you come over to say hi to me?"

"I was planning to, Blair. Let me introduce my new friends. Holly, Nina, and Jasper. Ladies and canine, Blair Blanning. Her older sister Becca and I are long-time buddies."

Blair looks at me. "Noah told me you're here from New York, to do some sort of story on the Salem Heritage House."

"That's right."

"When will you be coming by our vintage shop to pick up your costumes?"

"Costumes?" Holly and I look at one another.

"For the séance tomorrow night. Guests are expected to wear period dress."

I shake my head. "I'm sure Mr. Grant would have arranged for costumes if they expected it of us."

"It must have slipped his mind," Blair says. "I overheard my grandmother talking to him on the phone.

She asked me to find something suitable and put it aside for your visit. When are you bringing them by, Noah?"

"We're just putting a plan together now," he says, sounding flustered. This must have come as a surprise to him as well. "Holly, since you proposed a city tour, what do you say we start at 10:30 tomorrow and finish up at Blair's shop?"

"I'd love it," says Holly. "I can't wait to see Salem!"

As we leave the restaurant, Witch Wanda looks my way. Her eyes darken and narrow. It doesn't take a psychic to read her thoughts. *She doesn't like me.* I'd better be on my best behavior around her. *Who knows what kind of hex she might throw my way?*

CHAPTER 11

*H*olly and Noah stroll in front of me on the short walk back to the hotel. Every so often, their hands brush against each other. The electricity I imagine in their touch reminds me of Brad Collins. It can't be a mere coincidence that Brad and I have connected again after so many years.

As we approach the Salem Heritage House, I look up at our suite, which is centered above the main entrance. *Henrietta's suite.*

It's easy to visualize the beautiful Henrietta of two hundred years ago. In my mind's eye, she stands at the window, looking down at Salem Harbor with her long auburn hair tousled by the passing wind.

As if in response to my thoughts, a bright circle of light appears in the window.

"Holly. Do you see that light? It's coming from our room."

"Yes." Holly turns from me to Noah. "What does it mean?"

"Oh, that's just Henrietta Hawkins," says Noah, as if

the glowing light in our suite window is the most natural thing in the world.

"What do you mean? Explain, please."

"The ghost of Henrietta Hawkins has materialized in that window for centuries. That was her bedroom."

"When was the first time you saw Henrietta's ghost?"

Noah scratches his head. "I must have been five or six. We kids used to come here every so often. We tried throwing rocks at her window to make her come down to us, but Old Man Moses chased us away."

"Moses? The caretaker?"

Noah nods. "He was younger back then, of course. He *must h*ave been. But then my mom said the same thing happened when she was a kid."

I do the simple math. "Moses would have been pretty young himself back then."

"It could have been Moses's father," Noah says. "As far back as anyone can remember, there's always been a Moses B. Anthony guarding the property—all the way back to the minute old Captain Hawkins passed away."

I study Noah. What he's saying sounds crazy, but instinctively, I feel I can trust him. "I'm not one to put stock in ghosts, Noah. But today when I took a shower in our suite, I swear Henrietta's figure took form in the mist. Then her ghostly shape floated over to her portrait and faded into it."

Holly nods. "And I believe Nina saw her, even though I didn't see her myself."

"Noah, *why* does she haunt? Is there anything we can do for her?"

He shrugs. "I don't think ghosts need a reason to haunt. But lots of folks in Salem think her apparition is tied up with Captain Hawkins' treasure."

"Treasure?" Holly says.

"You bet, treasure. Salem sea captains like Hawkins don't risk their lives going out to sea to return empty handed. Folks say the treasure's stashed right here in this house."

"Surely people in town have tried to break in and find it over the years," I say.

Noah laughs. "Yes. But no one's been able to get past Moses. My mother told me that when she was a little girl, the cops found a would-be treasure hunter blabbering like an idiot outside the Salem Heritage House. Whatever he saw inside spooked him so bad he lost his mind."

"What spooked him?" I ask.

"Moses, presumably," Noah says. "My mom was always frightened of him. Said her grandmother heard he came from a long line of shamans back in whatever country Captain Hawkins found him in."

"Shaman?" Holly asks.

"They're kind of like witches," I say.

"Then why would he work like a servant in Captain Hawkins' house today?" she asks.

"According to Captain Hawkins' very public will," Noah says. "Moses' forbearer and his descendants were commissioned to act as *caretakers* of the estate. Caretaker, not servant."

"So Moses and his ancestors received payment for chasing treasure hunters and kids away from the house," Holly says, shaking her head. "Doesn't make much sense. Even if Moses made a good living wage, why would he stay?"

"Good point," I say. "Likely Moses feels an affinity or connection to the house. I saw it in his eyes. Even when Mr. Grant demanded that he clean up the glass from the fallen chandelier, Moses carried himself with dignity. Almost like he was the owner of the property."

I turn to Noah. "Do you think Moses knows where the treasure is buried?"

"If anyone knows, he might be the one," Noah says, yawning. "But we're not going to figure it out tonight." Noah kisses each of us on the cheek and shakes Jasper's paw. "Goodnight, ladies. See you in the morning. And goodnight, Mr. Jasper."

The Salem Heritage House is quiet as we enter. Holly seems oblivious to the way Henrietta observes us from the prison of her portrait as we climb up the stairwell. But I sense her gaze.

"We're home." I cautiously open the door to our suite, alert for ghosts and orbs of light. But there's nothing to be seen.

"I know it's your turn. But can I sleep with Jasper tonight?" Holly asks. "Or maybe we can all sleep together in the same bed—the way we did when we were kids."

"Did Henrietta's ghost story scare you?"

"Yes."

"Then take The Jasp. As if *he's* going to protect you. I'm fine sleeping alone." But as soon as I say the words, Pyewacket slithers through the open window and settles on my pillow.

"That cat," Holly says. "How did she get here?"

"She probably climbed the tree."

"Maybe the cat's a ghost, too."

"Maybe."

After preparing for bed, I snuggle into the crisp white cotton covers. Pyewacket lowers her velvet-textured paw onto the scar on my temple and purrs.

From her own bed, Holly snores. Jasper soon matches her rhythmic breathing with snorts of his own.

As I drift off to sleep, the image of Henrietta from her portrait floats into my mind. *What does she want with me?*

CHAPTER 12

J fall asleep easily enough. But an hour later, I'm
caught in some distant realm, neither awake nor
asleep. Images of the last several hours turn through my
mind like pages in a book.

Captain Hawkins greeting me at the train station.
Henrietta laughing at me though the imprisoning gold
frame of her portrait. Brad Collins' bright smile and the
way he looked at me with his mesmerizing blue eyes.

And then Moses, his ruby earring glittering as he
narrows his eyes at me, his gaze burning through my soul.

My eyes snap open. I gasp for breath.

Pyewacket twists her neck to gaze at me. She places a
warm paw on my shoulder.

"I'm okay, Pyewacket."

But I'm *not* okay. I've always found it hard to sleep after
disturbing dreams. I didn't come to Salem for ghosts, but
they haunt me. At least Henrietta does, if you call her
vaporous appearance a haunting.

Noah believes her spirit is alive. *But what does she want
with me?*

Outside the window, a near full moon hangs in the black velvet sky. Gazing toward my bed, I can almost make out my figure sleeping peacefully beneath the sheets.

Am I awake or asleep?

I rise. Pyewacket brushes against my ankles and scampers toward the closed door. I open it for her.

She darts out, but looks over her shoulder at me, as if expecting me to follow along. *Or daring me to.*

Shadows obscure the faces in the ancestral portraits as I follow Pyewacket down the stairs. When I reach Henrietta's portrait near the bottom step, her eyes gleam in satisfaction. Pyewacket leads me through the same secret passageway Brad showed me earlier. I shine my phone's light on the stairs and meet the cat's remarkable jewel-toned eyes as she ensures I'm following her.

On the second-floor landing, Pyewacket pushes herself against the door to Captain Hawkins' study, releasing the hidden spring.

Now well past midnight, the study appears darker and more ominous than it did with Brad. The near-full moon shines down from the skylight, casting eerie shadows against the walls. Moonlight also illuminates the spines of the books on the shelves—books I yearned to open and examine earlier with Brad. One of them may hold the mystery of why Henrietta haunts—and why the treasure has not yet been found.

But which of them holds the secret? There must be hundreds.

I allow my fingers to trace the hard leather spines of the books, feeling them for a sense of energy.

One thick book grabs my attention. Picking it up, I flip to the title page. *Les Liaisons Dangereuses* by Pierre Choderlos de Lacios—not a book you'd expect in the collection of a wealthy Salem sea captain.

The shelf of books below it appears more rustic. One

is particularly crudely bound, with frayed parchment at the spine. As I gently pry it from its neighbors, Pyewacket meows at my feet.

When I turn to the first page, a finely rendered sketch jumps out at me. *It's the spitting image of Moses.* Taking the fragile book in my hand, I move to one of the red velvet chairs along the wall. Shining my light over the first page, I can see the book is written in English. But it's the English you see in old documents—the letters *f* and *s* appear almost identical.

I carefully turn the ragged pages, focusing on the illustrations because it's so hard to decipher the words. One image shows the figure of a white man in an 18th-century outfit. *Pirate or sea captain?* It's difficult to tell.

A dark-skinned native appears to be showing the sea-faring man a gold mine at gunpoint. In the next illustration, a swirl of demons surround the white man, who wears an expression of abject horror. Each illustration after that offers a horrifying look at how the demons torture the foreigner, with some clawing out his eyes while others gnaw at his exposed intestines.

Even though the text is difficult to decipher, I can't resist reading what the ghastly illustration explains. According to the passage, the book tells the story of the Jharkhand people, who fought back with witchcraft when foreigners attempted to steal their gold. One caption reads: *Beware the dark forces, the shadows that come to life when summoned by the true master…*

What does that mean? And why does Captain Hawkins have this abhorrent book in his library? I'm torn between placing the book with its terrible illustrations back on the shelf and taking it with me to decipher its significance in the full light of day. Would that be stealing?

I may never have the chance to visit Captain Hawkins' study again.

My heart pounds as I make my way down the secret passageway with the book, passing through the kitchen and to the stairwell. As I pass by Henrietta's portrait, her bright eyes glow. Her lips turn upward in a smile, as if to say, *Yes, Nina. You're on the right track.*

CHAPTER 13

*A*fter a restless night, I awaken to something rough and wet against my cheek, followed by a firm tap on my shoulder from a soft paw.

Jasper.

The Jasp lets forth the same sharp *yip* he emits every morning in New York. It's Jasper-speak to make sure he gets his water bowl refreshed, a cuddle, and something crunchy to munch.

"Okay, Jasp. Let's see what Holly brought for you."

I walk to Holly's suitcase and move my hands through her things. Spools of thread, needles, and trim for Jasper's doggy outfits pop out at me from every direction. But there are none of his special-ordered canned meals. Just specialty canine chews and treats.

"Don't worry, Jasper." I break a crunchy doggy bone in half and feed it to him. "I'll find you something yummy and be back in a jiffy."

In the shower, I let warm water stream through my hair while I apply lilac-scented cleansing gel to my body. The luxurious marble of the refurbished bathroom offers an excellent teaser for what the rest of the Salem Heritage House could be like when it's finished.

I can visualize how appealing this small luxury inn will look in our magazine's pages. I'll really need to charm Mr. Pinkley when I meet him again tonight at the séance. The advertising contract needs to happen. The security of my mom's future relies on it.

After my shower, I dress and make my way to the kitchen. In the refrigerator, I find a giant container of Greek yogurt. *Perfect.* Jasper adores it.

As I turn away, yogurt in hand, I'm surprised by Brad, radiating health and energy, clear blue eyes gleaming.

Grinning, I hold up the yogurt container. "Just grabbing breakfast for Jasper."

Brad's smile fades. "Jasper, huh?"

The way he says it makes me think he believes Jasper's my boyfriend. "Oh, yes." I lay it on thick. "Jasper demands a hearty breakfast, especially after such a stimulating evening."

"You brought your man with you?"

"Jasper's my dog, not my boyfriend." I laugh. "Is it okay if I take this up for him?"

Brad nods and his smile returns. "What else does he like? I'm well stocked here. I have some rotisserie chicken with the skin and bones removed. Filet mignon. How about I wrap them up for you?"

"That would be great. Thanks."

I sit as Brad wraps the meat neatly in foil. He pulls a beautiful China plate from the cabinet and tucks it into a bag with the food.

"What's your plan for the day?" I ask him.

"Pinkley asked that I prepare dinner for the guests at the séance. But come join me on a jog this morning— nothing quite like a lap around the wharf in the fresh air."

"I'm meeting Holly and her friend at ten thirty."

"We'll be back well before then."

"Okay. Why not?" I take the food from Brad's hands. "I'll feed The Jasp and be right down."

After setting out the meal for Jasper, I put on a warm sweater and grab my tennis shoes. Holly is still snoring away as I steal down the hall.

When I open the front door, a blast of crisp air slaps my face. The sun's shining, though, making the falling leaves look like spun gold. I'm still enjoying the bliss of this scintillating new day when a loud squawk assaults my ears. When I turn, Brad approaches with Rico perched on his shoulder.

"Good morning, Nina," he says.

"Aye, top of the morning to you, my pretty," Rico adds, his dilated right eye leering at me. "*Dead men tell no tales.*"

I step back. I know I shouldn't be frightened by the ramblings of a one-pound bird, but Rico terrifies me. "What did he say?"

"Parrot language for wishing you good morning."

"Right. But what about that *dead men* thing?"

"Who knows? He's a smart old bird. I never met the sailor who owned him, but you can bet they shared many adventures together. Shall we go?"

I cross my arms over my chest. How can I tell Brad three's a crowd, even if one of them is a bird? "Will he *beak* me again?"

"No. He was just testing you out. Today's a new day. Right, Rico?"

"Today's a new day. Today's a new day," Rico croaks in a rhythmic beat, like a rapper. Perched on Brad's shoulder, he bobs his head and shimmies to his own beat.

I take a deep breath. But before I can speak, I notice the backpack on Brad's shoulders.

"What's that?"

"A surprise." He flashes that impish grin. Then we're off.

Brad leads me on a gentle jog down Essex Street, then turns past a sign that says *Pickering Wharf.* After running along the wharf, he guides me to a bank of grass overlooking the majestic old-fashioned sailing ships.

As soon as we're stationary, Rico flies from Brad's shoulder.

"Don't you need to catch him?"

"He'll be back. That bird can take care of himself." Brad reaches into his bag to pull out a picnic blanket.

"Can't beat the scenery." I point to the largest of the ships in the wharf. "What's the history of that vessel?"

"It's a replica of the three-masted, square-rigged *East Indiamen*—the merchant ship that helped Salem open international trade with the Far East. And here's what the original looked like." Brad flips through the pictures on his phone, then hands it to me, revealing a pen-and-ink drawing. "I based the sketch of the ship on an oil painting in Captain Hawkins' study."

"You're a man of many talents." I always knew Brad possessed many fine qualities. Handsome, of course. Determined? You bet. A genius with cuisine, but an artist too. "Whatever you're unwrapping smells delicious," I add, salivating as Brad arranges food on antique China plates.

"Behold cornbread—real pilgrim cornbread, spiked with sage from my garden. And lobster salad with labiatae."

"What's labiatae?"

"I showed it to you in my garden. It's a bit like catnip. But humans go crazy for it, too."

Brad prepares a plate for me.

I take a small bite of the lobster. "This is delicious. Did you steam it with the herbs?"

He nods. "That's how I roll."

"I should have known you were the mystery chef when you sent up those appetizers with the Champagne. You made your name with herb-infused lobster." I taste the other food on my plate. "I'm impressed, Brad. I never knew the pilgrims had it so good. The Early American cuisine is wonderful. If you're looking for a PR agent, give me a ring."

"Really? Would you consider it?"

"I was joking."

"You'd be a terrific PR agent, Nina. You have a great work ethic. I remember how you used to hustle back at the restaurant." Brad falls silent as he pours us tea from the thermos he brought. Then he looks at me. "I'm glad you joined me this morning." He puts his hand near mine. Not quite close enough to touch, but I feel its vibration. "I thought about you all last night."

"What were you thinking?"

"How lucky I am to have a second chance with you."

I laugh without meaning to. "I wasn't aware of the first chance."

"When we were working together, I always found you attractive. But I was your boss. You were a kid. And back then, I was obsessed with the restaurant, anyway."

"And now?"

Brad flashes his famous grin. "Now I'd say the playing field is level."

CHAPTER 14

Sitting on the grass overlooking Salem Harbor, I want this moment to last forever. Brad and I sip our tea in silence.

"You haven't changed, you know," he says after a moment. "Everything about you is the same—your long, wavy auburn hair, your casual, laid-back style, even that heart-shaped locket." He reaches over to touch it. "I remember that from the restaurant. I was always curious about the picture inside. I suspected it was some college boy."

"Nope. It's my parents. When they were young."

"May I?" He makes a move to open it.

I lean back so it's out of reach. "No. It's not something I share with people."

"I'm not a 'people,'" Brad says with a grin. "I'm your favorite chef, remember?"

"Why do you want to see them?"

"I want to know more about you, Nina. You're always so closed about your personal life. Even now, I know nothing about you except that you work at a foodie-centered luxury magazine. Do you have a boyfriend?"

"Did. Not anymore."

"Tell me about him."

For a moment, I consider gushing the details, all the agony and ecstasy of my time with Jean-Charles. But I'm betting he knows Jean-Charles, since he's a chef too. Then the questions will start—questions I don't have any interest in answering.

I shake my head. "No. But I'll show you the picture in my locket to satisfy your curiosity." I reach behind my neck to unclasp the gold chain. Then I take a deep breath and press the tiny lever, causing the gold-shaped heart to open. "That's Mom. And that's Dad."

My pulse quickens when Brad takes the locket into his large, calloused hands. "Attractive couple. But you don't look much like either of them."

"When I was little, people used to say I favored my dad. He had auburn hair like mine. He was a sharp dresser."

"Was?"

"He passed."

"I'm sorry."

"It was a long time ago."

"How old were you?"

"Brad, I didn't want to show you the picture in the first place. Can you please stop with the questions?"

He hands the locket back. "I'm sorry. I just want to know more about you. There's a lot to catch up on."

"I was seven," I say after a slight hesitation. "My father and I were taking a drive on Pacific Coast Highway. The sun danced on the ocean. I remember smelling the salty air, listening to my favorite song on the radio. Then there was a horrific noise."

"The next thing I knew, I was looking down at my body from high in the air. It seemed like I was in the clouds. And then I woke up in the hospital. Everyone came running in. Later they told me I'd been pronounced dead twenty minutes before."

Brad is silent for a moment. "Is that how you got your scar?"

My fingers fly to cover it. "Yeah. You'd think concealer, foundation, and long bangs would be enough to hide it, right?"

"Why try so hard? You can't erase that experience."

"I just tire of people asking about it all the time. When I conceal the scar, no one bothers me."

"Your mother is alive?" he asks after a moment.

I sigh. "Alive but ill. She's in her forties but was diagnosed with early Alzheimer's a few years ago. Most of the time she's fine—*almost* capable of caring for herself. But I hired a woman to look after her, Julep. She's a hoot, always taking snapshots and videos of Mom and sending them to me."

" So far, it's working out. Thanks to financial help from my elderly great-aunt, I've been able to keep Mom at home. But her estate lawyer isn't being clear about how long we can rely on this income. And he's suggested sending Mom to an institution to save on costs. I have no siblings and she's my sole responsibility."

"That must be a terrible burden."

"That's why I'm so disappointed with the situation at the Salem Heritage House. I had hoped the weekend would end in a lucrative advertising contract, yielding me a well-paid position on the marketing team. I need to make more money to care for Mom. Especially if or when—"

Tears flow unexpectedly. I hadn't realized how much I needed to share my fears.

Brad puts his arm around me. I relax at the warmth of his touch.

We're silent for a few moments until a spry, fashionable older woman in Lululemon yoga pants walks a neatly trimmed white poodle past us on the boardwalk. She looks more like a matron on Manhattan's Madison Avenue than a Salem tourist.

Brad excuses himself to speak to her for a moment.

"Who was that?" I ask when he returns.

"One of Salem's VIPs, Mrs. Blanning. She owns a vintage shop over on Derby Street, near the city center."

"Blair's mom? Grandmother?"

He shakes his head. "I don't know who Blair is, but Mrs. Blanning's a real foodie. She came to see me as soon as I arrived. She's totally on board with my Early American cuisine. I'm hoping she'll become one of my first investors."

The nearby church bells ring, announcing the hour.

"Thanks for bringing me here. But it's ten o'clock, so we'd better get back. I must meet Holly and Noah soon."

He nods. "Okay, but I'm supposed to meet Miss Lillian."

"Miss Lillian?"

"She's the head librarian at the Salem Library. Well, that was her title years ago. Now she's president emeritus and heads up the genealogical society—knows the skeleton in every family closet."

I cock an eyebrow. "Are you two going to dig up a grave?"

"She's giving me a cookie recipe."

"*Cookies?*"

"Yeah. I've been looking for a cookie recipe from the pilgrim era. She's been searching through the stacks and—"

"Stacks?"

"The old books in the basement. She texted me this morning that she found one so old it's handwritten on parchment. I'm going to prepare them for the séance tonight."

"Can I come? Maybe your Miss Lillian can help me with something."

"What is it?"

"Last night I couldn't sleep. I was curious to read those books you showed me in Captain Hawkins' study. So I took the secret passageway up to the library."

"Did you find anything good?"

"I think so. I found a super-old book, with an image of Moses' face inside it."

"Moses' face?"

I shrug. "Maybe it was Moses's relative, or someone who looked like him. But I couldn't read much of the text because of the peculiar lettering. Maybe Miss Lillian can explain what the book's about."

"I bet she could." He gathers our picnic items and places them inside his backpack.

"Do you think we'll see Captain Hawkins at the séance tonight?" I ask as he slips his backpack over his shoulders. "Do you believe in ghosts?"

"Why not? We'll all be ghosts one day, if we're lucky."

"Lucky?! What do you mean?"

"Ghosts have more fun," he says with a laugh. "Wouldn't you rather spend your afterlife playing practical jokes on the living? Or better yet, haunting them? Boo!"

I wrap my arms around myself, feeling a chill. "That's not funny."

"It's a joke, Nina. Where's all this coming from?"

I hesitate. I want to share that Henrietta's been manifesting herself to me. And ask why he thinks Captain

Hawkins came to meet me at the train station. But I worry he'd think I'm crazy, as looney as my mother.

Just then Rico swoops down, landing with a shriek on Brad's shoulder. As we walk back to Essex Street, I sense something behind me, then feel another strange chill.

When I turn, there's the ghost of Captain Hawkins. He smiles and tips his cap. "Until tonight."

CHAPTER 15

*S*alem's library, a classic, red-brick building, stands tall on tree-lined Essex Street. So many children crowd the steps, reading books we need to zigzag our way past them to enter.

As Brad opens the door, that familiar library scent wafts our way—a heady mix of old books, dust, and bologna sandwiches wilting inside paper lunch bags.

"This way." Brad passes the checkout librarians, walking with a confident stride toward the back offices. He pulls open an aged wooden door with a sign declaring *employees only* and we move toward an office at the end of the hall. The door stands slightly ajar. In what I remember as true Brad Collins style, he pushes it all the way open without knocking.

"Miss Lillian."

A tiny woman with a face as wrinkled as an apple-head folk doll beams up at us from behind her desk. She's gathered her deep brown hair, likely dyed or a wig, to the top of her head. Long bangs cover her forehead, while loose tendrils dance around her dainty ears.

"Brad." Her features animate into a broad smile. "You've brought a friend. Hello, dear. Welcome to the Salem library. I'm Lillian Cotten."

"Nina Brown. A pleasure to meet you." I stride forward to shake her hand. Though her grasp is firm, her fingers have the dry texture of parchment. Looking at her welcoming face, I find it impossible to estimate her age. *70s? 80s?*

The brown, gold, and red of her wildly colorful dress remind me of a Caribbean flag. She's piled so much shiny costume jewelry around her wrists and throat, she resembles a five-year-old just back from a shopping spree.

"Welcome, Nina." Beaming, she looks from me to Brad and back, as if she's pleased to see us together. "Brad, darling, I've set up the book of recipes in the private viewing room. Be careful with those fragile pages, you hear?"

"Yes, ma'am. I'll be a few minutes, Nina," he says with a saucy wink at Lillian. "Do you see what I have to do to score a simple cookie recipe here?"

"I'll take good care of her while you're gone." Lillian turns her full attention to me as Brad leaves the room.

"You are so lovely," she says. "And you look like such a *nice* person, too. Just what Brad needs."

"Thanks. We're old friends."

"Only friends? We'll see about that. Have a seat, dear. Tell me about yourself."

The "seat" is a giant, rainbow-colored beanbag chair before her desk—a time-travel icon from the swinging sixties.

"How do I sit on it?"

"Just plop yourself down, dear. It will conform."

I sit, rather gingerly, on the chair. Man, this hurts. It's

like each hard-as-heck bean is set on imprinting itself in my jeans-covered derriere.

"Tell me about yourself, Nina. What brings you to Salem?"

"I'm with *Travel! Food! Wine!* magazine. I heard Mr. Pinkley was turning the Salem Heritage House into a luxury inn, and I thought it would make a good story, so I'm here."

She nods. "It's certainly a good story. You're right. When I was a little girl, the Salem Heritage House was the subject of great mystery. Have you seen a ghost yet?"

The casual way Lillian says this surprises me. "A ghost?"

"Well, dear, this is Salem, after all. And this is Halloween. Given the circumstances, I'd be surprised if you hadn't seen a ghost."

"I'll be on the lookout," I say with a laugh. "Whose ghost should I watch for?"

"Most ghost sightings are of the dashing Captain Hawkins. Or dear Henrietta."

My eyes widen. "Have you seen them?"

Someone raps on the door.

"Come in," she calls.

The door opens, revealing the teenage witch Noah pointed out last night at the Flying Saucer pizza place. But today, instead of a rinky-dink synthetic witch outfit, she's wearing an eye-popping geometric dress with white, knee-high boots—a 1960s relic from her family's vintage shop, no doubt.

"Blair, I'm in a meeting," Lillian admonishes. "This is Nina Brown, from Manhattan."

"Hi, Nina!" Blair waves at me, then turns toward Lillian. "We met last night. Lillian, I need to borrow the key to the third quadrant archive."

Lillian shakes her head. "You know that's off limits, save for university scholars with a letter of recommendation."

The teen witch pouts. "I won't have those qualifications for decades. Please don't make me wait that long."

Lillian fake sighs with a little smile. It's clear she has some affection for the girl. "What do you plan to research, Blair?"

Blair glances in my direction, then moves toward Lillian to whisper in her ear.

Lillian shakes her head. "I'm sorry, but I can't allow that."

Blair rolls her eyes and stamps her foot like a petulant child. But she recovers quickly and smiles at me. "I hope you enjoy Salem, Nina. I look forward to seeing you at my shop later today."

Lillian and I wait to speak further until Blair closes the door behind her.

"What did she want to research?" I ask.

Lillian shakes her head. "That girl. She's wanted to be a full-fledged witch since she was three years old—started with the witchy picture books Salem librarians read during story time. Then she devoured our collection of young adult magical books. Now she wants to venture into our research vault."

"What does the vault hold?"

"What it *doesn't* hold is the better question. We have the largest collection of Wicca books from the 16th and 17th centuries in the world. Many of the parchment manuscripts detail the spells of witches who were burned at the stake. Powerful magic," she says with a shudder.

I take a moment to catch my breath. *Powerful magic in a public library? Where wanna-be teen witches like Blair Blanning can read the most potent spells? Maybe even put them into practice? And this frail lady is the gatekeeper? That doesn't seem adequate protection.* "Could someone use the spells to cause real harm?"

"Yes, dear. The spells and incantations in the manuscripts may be old, but never forget—their power has not diminished."

"You're not letting Blair in, right? Or anyone else? I know it's none of my business, but she seems a little too young to be playing with magic. Especially if it's as powerful as you say."

Lillian picks up a ring of keys from her desk. "Rest assured, dear. These keys stay with me at all times."

CHAPTER 16

I'm still enjoying my conversation with Lillian in her library office when her desk telephone rings. She excuses herself to take the call, and I use the time to look around her office.

Lillian's wooden desk is free of clutter, save for a container filled with finely sharpened colored pencils and markers. An old-fashioned cassette player sits on the credenza behind her, with two cassette tapes resting on top. Sea green walls give the room a relaxing ambiance, yet the most curious items are the animal heads mounted in each corner, including a lion, a bear, and a crocodile.

"Are those real?" I gesture to the taxidermy specimens after Lillian finishes her call.

"Of course. You think I'd hang decapitated plush animal toys on my walls?"

"Who shot them?"

"I did. Of course, we're talking a decade ago, when I was younger. The lion and bear I killed in self-defense on two separate occasions when we were under attack. Now the croc, I killed that one on a safari just two years ago—

with a knife, mano a mano, not a bullet," she adds proudly. "You can see a picture of the carnage right below its mounted head."

In the photo, Lillian sports green and gray camouflage gear, and she's holding a bloody knife as she stands beside the dead croc.

"Self-defense, of course. He was just a jaw snap away from gobbling up my colleague. Now, shall I give you the library tour?"

I nod, quickly checking my watch. I still have a few minutes. "I'd like that. But since you mentioned Henrietta, can we talk about her? And can we keep this confidential? I wouldn't want anyone to know."

"Why on earth not? Tourists visiting Salem pay good money to see a ghost."

"I'm not a tourist. I'm here to do a story. And I wouldn't want people to think I'm a little...*woo woo*."

Lillian looks at me. "What does that mean?"

"Crazy. Well, in Manhattan it does. Here in Salem, maybe it means you're just part of the community vibe."

"Fair enough. What's your question?"

"I'm staying in Henrietta's room at the Salem Heritage House. Earlier, you said people have seen her ghost."

"Yes. What about it?"

I hesitate. *Do I really want people to think I'm crazy?* But the way Lillian looks at me with her crisp blue eyes makes me feel sure she'll understand.

I decide to start slow and see where it takes me. "I wouldn't go as far as to say I've *seen* her ghost, but when I pass by her portrait, I feel a certain connection to her. Mr. Grant says I resemble her."

"You do resemble her." Lillian nods. "The likeness is uncanny."

I shrug. "I think it's just the auburn-hair-and-green-eyes combo. Plus, we're about the same age and petite."

"All this is true. Yet consider that it's no accident you're here in Salem for Halloween weekend. I'm no psychic, but something big is going to happen, and you're an integral part of it."

"What's going to happen?"

Lillian shrugs. "Not sure. But I'll bet you anything it will kick off at the séance tonight."

"You're coming to the séance?"

"Yes. Ernest Pinkley invited me personally. Wanda too. He's trying to make nicey-nice with the preservation committee—not that a dinner and a séance will do all that much to help his situation."

"But aren't you and Wanda the ones blocking the renovations?"

Lillian chooses her words carefully. "I wouldn't say we're *blocking* his renovations. We're *modern Salemites,* after all. We understand the value of progress. And we recognize that a fine balance exists between helping tourism grow and letting capitalism get out of hand."

"But I heard the preservation committee wouldn't allow any further renovation of the rooms—"

"Well, now, as a journalist, you must be the first to recognize that there are two sides to every story. In defense of the Salem Preservation Committee, I must inform you it's not a simple case of allowing or not allowing renovation of the rooms. There's much more to it than that." Lillian rises. "But let's not talk of that now. Brad asked me to show you the library. So show you the library, I shall."

Outside her office, Lillian begins her VIP tour. "The Salem Library is one of the oldest in Massachusetts, dating from 1855."

For a tiny lady, the librarian moves quickly. I race to keep up with her.

"I'll skip the main floor," she says. "It's like every circulating library you've seen since you were knee high. Let us climb the grand staircase so I can show you the Hall of Ten Families." Lillian unfastens one side of a velvet rope, blocking off the stairwell, and ushers me through.

"We open the stairwell and grand hall for town festivities—and VIPs. Otherwise, it's off limits to library patrons."

Like the stairwell at the Salem Heritage House, portraits of aristocratic people from previous centuries line the polished walnut walls as we climb.

Lillian deftly opens another red velvet rope at the top of the stairs. I cross through and enter a magnificent room. It looks more like part of a fancy, big-city museum than the second floor of a local library. Even more gold-framed portraits line the walls here. But one wall features an assortment of mostly black-and-white photographs. They're all the same dimensions, but the newer ones are in color.

"What is this?"

"Come," says Lillian. "I'll show you." Taking my hand, she brings me to the wall of photographs. "Here we've mounted pictures of the graduating class of Salem High School for the last one hundred and fifty years."

I spend a few moments looking at the class photos. The class of 2002 grabs my attention. "This boy looks so familiar."

"Sharp eyes. That's Ernest Pinkley."

I inspect the photo. He sported the same arrogant, condescending smirk even back then. The woman in the square class photo below him looks familiar too, especially with that trademark strip of white in her otherwise jet-black hair.

"That's Wanda Williams, isn't it?"

Lillian nods. "The two of them were an odd couple. I'll say that much."

"Who? Mr. Pinkley and Witch Wanda? They were dating?"

She shrugs. "No one quite knew if their relationship was romantic or not. But they were inseparable—and instantly recognizable wherever they went. Wanda, tall, dark, shapely, and so mysterious with her raven black hair and violet eyes. Then poor Ernest Pinkley, short and pudgy even in his adolescent prime."

"What do you think the attraction was between them?"

"No idea. But opposites attract, or so they say. Have you met Witch Wanda?"

I nod. "She gave me a psychic reading. It was scary how much she seemed to know about me."

"She is brilliant that way, isn't she? She's running for mayor of Salem, you know. Having a female mayor is nothing new—Kim Driscoll took the mayor's office back in 2006. But a *witch*, now that will be a first. Wanda certainly has enough energy to take the position. She's been like a little energizer bunny since she was a girl."

"You knew her then?"

"Of course. She had that streak of white in her hair as a toddler flipping through picture books at the children's table down below. Genetic chiaroscuro, they say. Then when Wanda turned twelve, she couldn't get enough of those witchcraft books."

"Sounds like Blair Blanning is on the same path."

Lillian laughs. "Possibly. Though Blair's what I call a 'lipstick witch'."

"Is that like a lipstick lesbian?" My words surprise me.

I'm not sure what a lipstick lesbian is, let alone a lipstick witch. When Lillian says nothing, I try again. "What does that mean, exactly?"

"I've always had the feeling Blair was *play acting* at being a witch. Like it was a way to call attention to herself—mostly because of her big sister, Becca."

"I met Noah Samuels yesterday. He mentioned that Blair's older sister was his good friend."

Lillian nods. "Becca was always number one in everything—star of the girls' volleyball team, straight-A student, then a scholarship to Harvard. Now she's getting her MBA at Cambridge University in England. Smart girl, that Becca."

"Blair always felt in her shadow?"

"You could say that. When she was a child, Blair liked to pretend she was a witch. She came out of it for a time as a preteen when acting in school plays became a thing."

"And now she's back into it."

"Teens," says Lillian with a laugh. "We'll see how long she sticks with it. Witchcraft is hard work. Exhausting, even. Blair seems to think all she has to do is wave a sparkly pink wand to make people do her bidding."

"How is Wanda's approach to witchcraft different?"

Lillian inclines her head, considering the question. "Wanda was always very *serious* about witchcraft. She started reading fortunes for tourists on Essex Street when she was just fifteen. Began wearing that athame like a gun holster, never taking it off. Then she started with the spells. And the voodoo."

"Voodoo?" The mere mention of that word sends chills down my spine. *Was it voodoo in that strange book I took from Captain Hawkins' library?*

"Yes. I think of it as her dark phase. Black magic. Then that horrible business about the German—"

I turn my attention away from Lillian as something small, black, and as fleeting as a shadow flashes across the half-open window. For a moment, I remember the horrific illustration of demons descending upon the seafarer's body, gnawing at his eyes and organs. Suddenly, I feel myself melding into that illustrated figure, feeling the attack of so many witchcraft-induced demons.

I can't help but shriek. And shriek again.

CHAPTER 17

When I open my eyes, I recognize the high, vaulted library ceiling and the large windows.

"Nina? Are you okay, dear?" Lillian peers into my face. "Here, you'd better sit down."

I fight to regain my breath as Lillian escorts me to an overstuffed green velvet chair.

"What was it you saw?" she asks.

"Something black, shadowy—but with life or animated by life." I look at the window. "There it is."

Lillian turns in the direction I point. Rising, she makes a *tsk* sound beneath her breath as she moves to the slightly open window. "That darn cat." Lillian slams the window closed.

"That was Pyewacket?"

Lillian nods. "Pyewacket isn't your average feline. I've known her since I was a child. She checks in with me at the library almost every day."

"Obviously it's not the same cat."

"Oh, it's Pyewacket, all right."

I'm not going to belabor the point. Quirky old people have their own ideas. "But there was something more. Last night I browsed the books in Captain Hawkins' library. I came upon one that must be over two hundred years old. The light was dim, though, and it was hard to read with its old English letters.

"What about the book?" she asks.

"Do you know Moses B. Anthony? The caretaker at the Salem Heritage House?"

She nods. "I know Moses. What about him?"

"His face was illustrated on the first page of the book."

"If the room was as dark as you said, maybe it wasn't Moses at all."

"If it's the Moses we're both thinking of you, must know he has a distinctive look. The elongated shape of his head, that aquiline nose. He even had that same ruby earring in his left ear."

"Moses has a distinctive look because he is descended from the people of Jharkhand. In small, cut-off communities like that, villagers share similar physical traits. That book you found might be about the witches of Jharkhand."

"You know the book?"

Lillian shakes her head. "No. But here in Salem, the murder of Captain Hawkins, the missing Jharkhand gold, and curse are usually spoken about in the same sentence. For a journalist, you certainly came to Salem unprepared."

I'm too polite to remind Lillian that I came to Salem because of a luxury hotel, not to delve into curses, gold, or murder. "What is this curse?"

Lillian shrugs. "Your basic curse on any treasure. Anyone who finds the treasure will be killed."

"In the book I found, a man—I'm not sure if he was a pirate or the captain of a chartered ship—was tormented by demons shortly after he tried to claim the gold."

"Well, there you have it then," she says with a shrug. "Shall we continue with the tour?

I follow Lillian's trim figure as she strides across the highly polished wooden library floor. On the wall at the end of the hall hangs an enormous portrait.

"Behold, Henrietta." Miss Lillian whispers the word like the name of a good friend.

"I've counted three portraits of Henrietta in the Salem Heritage House so far," I say. "One's on the staircase, one's in my room—I'm staying in Henrietta's suite—and another is in Captain Hawkins' study. She appears different in all three of them. And this one here is different still."

Lillian nods as if she knows just what I mean. "Captain Hawkins commissioned the lovely portrait in your room when Henrietta was just sixteen. I don't have a solid recollection of the portrait by the stairs. But in this picture before you now, she's twenty and the mother of a young son."

"How do you know the portrait in my room? I was told the Salem Heritage House had been boarded up for two hundred years."

Lillian laughs. "It's a rite of passage for children here to break into the Salem Heritage House every Halloween. I enjoyed my fair share of trespassing fun when I was a child —and as an adult on more than a few occasions."

I look up at the portrait of Henrietta with her newborn son. This time, she doesn't meet my eyes. "She doesn't look very happy."

"Not surprising. What a hard life Henrietta led, losing her parents at sea as a young girl. Thank God she had

Captain Hawkins to give her a home and make her his ward."

"How old was she when the shipwreck killed her parents?"

"Sixteen, according to the existing records."

"Captain Hawkins looks relatively young in his portraits. Do you think he was in his early thirties at the time?"

"About that age, yes."

"Why do you think he didn't just marry her? Sixteen was a typical age for a girl to wed in those days. And a fifteen-year age difference between husband and wife was common."

"That's a question history never answered, at least in the records I can access in this library. But it's common knowledge that Captain Hawkins' first love was the sea. It's possible he didn't want to marry Henrietta and leave her alone while he sailed. Maybe he thought she deserved a better life with a different man."

"Who did she eventually marry?"

Lillian's lips tighten. "A local boy," she says, continuing after a brief hesitation. "A ne'er do well. I don't like to repeat sad stories, but if you don't know already, I suppose you'll find out tonight during the séance. Henrietta's husband hired two killers to murder Captain Hawkins."

"Why?"

"To claim his property and find the treasure, or a map leading to it. But they found nothing. Captain Hawkins survived the attack, lingering for ten days before his death. He must have been certain Henrietta's husband orchestrated his attempted murder because he dictated a new will."

"In it, he cut Henrietta and her husband out of his

fortune. He indicated that upon his death, the Salem Heritage House would close for two centuries, with the newly created Salem Preservation Committee responsible for its upkeep. Now that the centuries have passed, according to the will, Mr. Hawkins' oldest living descendant could claim the house and assets found in it."

"By *assets* you mean the treasure, right?'"

"If there *is* a treasure. And that's a big if. Only old Salem gossip suggests Captain Hawkins even found one."

"How does Moses figure into this?"

Lillian shakes her head. "All I know is what's written in the library archives.

There's always been a Moses B. Anthony protecting Captain Hawkins' home. Even when I was a kid. Now let's continue."

Lillian grasps my arm, leading me toward the arched opening into the next room. As we approach, Brad walks toward us, with Rico perched on his shoulder.

"I've been looking for you. Miss Lillian, that cookie recipe is exactly what I've been hoping for." He bows low. "Thank you."

"Rico wants a cookie. Rico wants a cookie," the bird says.

"You're welcome, Brad. And don't get your feathers in a ruffle, Rico. I'm sure Brad will give you your share. I was just taking Nina to the archive."

"Actually, I think this is all I have time for today," I tell her. "I promised Noah and my roommate I'd join them for a Salem tour."

"Ah, Noah. Splendid young man. Come, then. This way."

Miss Lillian walks us to the library door. "You look good together," she says one last time.

I watch as Brad and Lillian exchange a warm hug.

Outside the library, Brad sparks tingles over my body when he puts his hand on mine. But a chill soon follows as I consider the séance I must attend tonight. *Something is going to happen. I know it. And it won't be good.*

CHAPTER 18

*B*rad pulls me down the library steps, leading me to an old-fashioned, green-painted sidewalk bench. For a moment, I feel like I'm caught in a time warp to small-town America, or trapped in a Hallmark card.

A three-dimensional, movie-like montage where I can see, smell, hear, and feel everything before me. My eyes take in the library steps, still littered with gossiping schoolchildren, the skeletal gray trees, and the chilly air biting at our exposed ears.

Brad puts his hand on my jeans-covered knee. I enjoy the comforting warmth for a quick moment before Rico squawks. *"Hands off the lady! Hands off the lady!"*

Then my cell phone vibrates. My anxiety rises as I look at the caller ID. My phone settings allow exclusively two numbers to get through to me over the weekend—my mom and her helper, Julep, or my boss, Ruth Ross.

"I need to take this," I say, walking away from the bench to give Brad the chance to discipline his bird.

This time it's Ruth. *Trouble.*

"Nina, darling." Ruth's voice flows over my ears,

99

smooth as honey, when I answer. "How are you enjoying your weekend in Salem?"

"Everything's moving along well." A lie, but no need to rock the boat just yet.

"And the Salem Heritage House? As divine as you suggested in your pitch?"

"Yes. And there's money to be had here in advertising. But—"

"But what? They're not going to advertise?" Ruth's voice loses its honey.

"Oh, they will. *They will.* Just not in the timeframe I pitched. They're not as far along in their process as they led me to believe. So, I've temporarily moved to Plan B."

"And what is that?" Ruth's voice is flat-out hard now.

"Our new feature story. A classic American saga about the rise and—"

Before I can continue, the booming voice of our owner and CEO, Marvin Roseman, comes through the phone as he enters Ruth's office.

"Look, Nina, I'll have to call you back." With that, Ruth ends the call with a sharp click.

"Bad news?" Brad is at my side as soon as I'm off the call.

"My boss."

"Bad news. Bad news," croaks Rico.

We both laugh.

"Have you met Ruth Ross?" I ask him.

"Back in the day, sure. She was always trying to get into my pants."

"You're kidding."

"No. For real. All the foodies were trying to seduce me—journalists, housewives, even houseboys. You name it."

"Why didn't you take Ruth up on it? She's certainly

attractive enough. And she could have done wonders for your career."

He shakes his head. "I didn't need her. I did wonders for my career on my own."

"So, you did." I sigh. "I need to string her along until the Salem Heritage House is ready to advertise. I'm going to pitch her a new story. And I need you to be part of it."

Brad laughs. "*Need?*"

"Yes. I'm going to feature your life journey and how it's culminated with your new restaurant serving pilgrim food."

"Early American cuisine."

"Right. I can see the cover of *Travel! Food! Wine!* magazine. You'll be dressed in starched chef's whites, holding a pot of… Just what will you be holding, Brad?"

"Fiddleheads."

"Yes. *That.* But what are fiddleheads?"

"The furled heads of a young fern."

"Sounds delicious. Actually, *not really.* We'll have to think of something a bit more appetizing."

"We have time," he says as Holly rushes toward us.

Brad slips his hand into mine and massages my palm with the pad of his thumb. Insanely delicious sensations dance over me. "I have a few fiddleheads lurking in my larder to show you," he whispers.

"Hey, Nina. Glad I found you," Holly says, cuddling Jasper in her arms. "Noah's about to give us his tour." Then she looks up, acknowledging Brad. "Oh. Hi. You must be the cute celebrity chef I've heard about."

Rico gives Holly the once-over with his black-rimmed eye. *"Fiddlehead. Fiddlehead."*

"Brad, I'd like you to meet my best friend and roommate, Holly Broad. And this is our Frenchie, Jasper."

"Holly." Brad rolls her name around on his tongue. "I remember Nina mentioning you back at La Toque. And

Jasper. Always a pleasure to meet a gentleman who understands the art of dressing well."

Today Jasper is decked out in what Holly calls a "leisure suit" in her online doggy portfolio. It comprises a tan slip-on jacket with an attached white open-necked shirt and white cuffs. *For the relaxed pooch,* Holly wrote in the advertising copy.

Jasper yips happily. Then he pivots so his rear end faces Brad. He gives Brad what Holly and I call the "bum wiggle."

"What the heck is he doing?" Brad asks, laughing. "Should I be insulted?"

"He's showing his affection," says Holly. "It's Jasper's way of saying *hi. Nice to meet you.*"

"French Bulldogs don't have much of a tail," I explain. "So Jasper wags his booty instead."

"Wag your booty! Wag your booty!" says Rico, bopping to his own beat on Brad's shoulder.

I turn to Holly. "Where is Noah?"

"He's in the Halloween parade. But he's going to part from them when he reaches the library. Can you hear them?"

The sound of trumpets and drums soon herald the parade's arrival. Noah marches in the first row. He's dressed as an 18th-century pirate with tan breeches, a red sash around his waist, and a gold-buttoned navy-blue coat. Thrust inside his sash is a short sword. A three-cornered black hat sits at a jaunty angle on his head.

Seeing us, Noah breaks away from his fellow marchers. "Pirate Noah Samuels at your service." He bows low before us.

"Hey, Noah. You're looking sharp." Brad clasps his hand.

I look at Brad. "You two know one another?"

"Salem's a small town," says Brad. "Noah, will you wear this as your costume for the séance tonight?"

"Yep. I've worn it every Halloween since I was a little kid. See this cutlass?" He gestures to the short sword at his waist. "My mother gave it to me for Halloween when I was five, and I've been wearing it on Halloween ever since."

"How's a cutlass different from a sword?" Holly asks.

"It's shorter, with a curved blade. A sword has a long blade with a hilt."

Brad taps the chef's knife he wears slung low around his waist. "I've been wearing mine since age sixteen, when Chef David entrusted it to my care."

"Chef David. The first US Michelin-rated chef?"

Brad nods. "He knew he was seriously ill. Out of all the chefs he mentored, he wanted me to have it. It's been my good luck charm ever since."

"Nice, but mine's bigger." Noah laughs as he unsheathes his cutlass, holding it up in the air. "Hardy har har."

Brad deploys the knife and playfully crosses it with Noah's cutlass.

"Ooh, it's sharp." Noah withdraws his weapon, frowning as he inspects a nick on the blade.

"It's sharp because my vegetables demand it. Precise cutting is rooted in the blade's angle." Brad spins his knife with the showmanship of a sushi master before tucking it safely back into the holster.

"I'm glad I'm not one of your vegetables." I shiver. Sharp objects always make me apprehensive.

"Excuse me. Now I need to get back to the galley—I mean kitchen," Brad says with a wink. "Until tonight."

We wave goodbye, and Noah slips into tour-guide mode as he prepares to show Holly and me the old buildings in Salem center. But as we walk, I feel strangely unsettled. *Is it because of the swordplay?*

"What's wrong, Nina?" Holly touches my arm. "Are you okay?"

Even Jasper looks at me with concerned eyes.

"Sure. I'm fine." I flash them a reassuring smile. But I still have a sense of foreboding about what the night will hold.

CHAPTER 19

The sun peeks out from the clouds to brighten the Salem streets as Noah begins the grand tour. We walk from the sidewalk in front of the library to Essex Street, its vibrant throng of tourists eager to kick off Halloween night with a bang.

"This is where we had dinner last night." Holly points. "Flying Saucer Pizza is just across the street."

"It looks different in the daytime, right? Not as scary." Noah does his version of an evil monster and waggles his fingers in the air.

Holly laughs, and even Jasper manages a polite snort. But to me, Essex Street isn't scary at all, night or day. It's just a cookie-cutter tourist trap you'd see anywhere in the world, marked by McDonalds, postcard displays, and hat shops with a tarot-reading table tossed in for good measure.

I sigh. "Noah, will you have time to show us the *real* Salem? *Pretty please?* If you don't, my Salem-focused story will fall apart."

"There's not much of old Salem left to see," he says

with a shrug. "But I'll show you my family's old candy shop."

We cross the intersection and turn onto the historic street. Noah points to the small, traditional brick buildings. "This block is still relatively untouched from when it was created a few centuries ago."

Derby Street doesn't seem as touristy as Essex Street, but it groans with rundown shops offering kitschy trinkets.

"Is the city going to renovate the area?" I ask.

Noah turns to me, rubbing his fingertips together in the international gesture for money. "They'd like too. But no moolah. And that sucks, because it almost paves the way for money-grubbing developers to buy it all up on the cheap."

"But they can't tear down classic buildings like this to build new structures, can they?" I ask. "Wouldn't that go against the preservation laws?"

"Supposedly." Noah's lips tighten. "But money makes anything possible. Here's my family's candy shop, on the right."

"That's the cute shop where I bought candy for Nina's mom," says Holly. "I can't believe your family owned it, Noah."

I look through the window into the interior. The shop bustles with a half dozen excited children bouncing around.

"I can just see you running around in a sugar rush like that." I laugh. Every time I look at Noah, I see the little kid living within him.

He shakes his head. "I couldn't play. I was helping my mom make the candy in the back."

"Where is she now?"

"Boston," Noah says, after a slight pause. "She's ill. Right now, it's a race against time."

"What do you mean?" Holly asks.

"I'm trying to get the candy shop back in the family while she's still alive. The doctors can't tell me how much longer she has, but they have said she's lost the *will* to live. I'm certain if I'm able to buy back the candy shop, it will give her some spark again."

"Did you try for a bank loan?" I ask.

"No. Like I said last night, the owner refuses to sell."

"Maybe if the price was right…

"No, Nina. He's an evil developer determined to buy up Salem. It started with our family candy store a decade ago. Slowly but surely, he's snatching up other properties, too. He has to be stopped." Noah's voice rises to a shout.

Startled by his outburst, Holly and I look at each other. Jasper buries his face in the crook of Holly's arm.

"I'm sorry, ladies. I didn't mean for it to come out like that. Apologies, Jasper." Noah rubs our pooch behind his ears. "But I just spoke to the doctor again today. The news gets worse and worse."

"I'm sorry, Noah." Holly takes his hand. "Is there anything we can do to help?"

Noah shakes his head. He takes a deep breath, and in a moment, his normally sunny countenance returns. "Let's check in with Blair at her vintage shop about the costumes."

He leads us down the street to a small, two-story building with a whitewashed wood exterior and bright red geraniums planted in windowsill pots. By far, it's the nicest looking building on the block.

In the storefront window, three mannequins stand dressed for an 18th-century masquerade. Above the doorframe is the store's name: *Yes, It's Real.*

As Noah pushes the door open, a bell chimes. I detect the heady scent of frangipani incense mingled with mothballs. Blair Blanning stands smiling before us, still wearing that 1960s geometric number with the white go-go boots.

"Blair, nice to see you." Noah embraces her, kissing her once on each cheek. "You remember Nina, Holly, and Jasper."

"Of course. Why don't you all make yourselves comfortable in the lounge while I bring up the selections? You'll find hot tea in the samovar."

Blair disappears, and the three of us move toward a cozy grouping of red velvet chairs. Then we take tea in real China cups while Holly pours Jasper fresh water.

Tea in hand, I observe the small, black-and-white family photographs on the shop wall.

"Noah, who is this woman?" I ask after a moment. "I saw her this morning on an early jog with Brad."

"That's Blair's grandmother, Mollie. Gracious lady."

"And these young women in white?" I point to several daguerreotype-style photographs.

"Not sure. Hookers likely," Noah says with a little laugh. "This place was the biggest bordello in town in its day."

"Bordello?" Holly raises her eyebrows.

"Sure. Ships were always pulling in and out of port. Sailors wanted female companionship after their long voyages."

I look at the women in the pictures. One of them, with dark eyes and hair, catches my gaze. Her dress looks extra racy for that era, with its sweetheart neck and lace-up, corset-like bodice.

She looks so familiar. *Why?*

*a*fter a few minutes, we hear Blair's light, energetic steps reverberating as she climbs back up to the main floor of the shop.

"This is what I found for you ladies," she announces. "Genuine antiques. Would you like to try them on?"

Blair holds a dress in each hand. They're floor length, tightly fitted, and fussy with bows, tiny buttons, and ribbons all over them. One is red and decadent, with a corset-like bodice, and the other is white and modest.

"I think this white one will look fabulous on you, Nina. I'll put it in this dressing room here. And this red dress will bring out your black hair and eyes, Holly. I'll place it in that red changing room there."

Holly nods, and we disappear into our respective dressing rooms. Mine is the size of a small shower enclosure.

I remove my clothes and step into the dress with care. The fabric seems so fragile. Like most 18th-century dresses I've seen in museums, the bodice narrows at the waist, and the skirt flares out from hips to ankles.

"Nina, you look fabulous." Noah says when I emerge from my small dressing area to the larger room.

Blair claps her hands. She seems genuinely excited. "Gorgeous. You can be a ghost from that era, especially since the dress is white."

I shake my head. "That's a scary thought. Blair, has anyone bought a dress here and told you it was haunted?"

"The entire shop is haunted." Blair laughs brightly. "Does that bother you?"

"Uh…no."

"You don't say that with much conviction," she says. "But why would it bother you? Ghosts like to stay close to the things and people they loved when they were alive."

Oddly, that makes sense to me. "Every item of clothing you have here has a ghost attached?"

"Maybe not every *single* piece. But most. Now let me see if some adjustments are needed."

"Wait. I don't have an expense account for this trip. How much is this dress?"

"No worries," says Blair. "I'll give it to you on loan. You can bring it back before you leave town. Now, stand straight right here, Nina, before the mirror."

I focus on my reflection as Blair tugs at the dress.

"It's amazing, Nina. The dress fits as if custom-made for your body. I don't need to do a thing."

"I look like that portrait of Henrietta at the Salem Heritage House."

"You do indeed," Blair says.

"You've seen it?"

Noah laughs. "Oh, Blair's seen it, all right. Becca, Blair, me, and a half dozen other kids have broken into the house every Halloween for years."

"Lillian told me she did the same thing when she was a child. Did Moses chase you away?"

"Sure. That's part of the fun," Blair says with a laugh. "We all knew he wouldn't really do anything to us."

I hear a rustling sound from Holly's dressing room, and a moment later, she sweeps aside her red velvet curtain to pose dramatically for us. "Behold the bombshell," she announces.

The dress cinches in Holly's waist, accentuating her large bosom.

I turn from her to the black-and-white photos on the wall. "Blair, do you see the girl in that photo on the bottom right? She looks like she's wearing the dress Holly wears now. Is this dress from the days this place was a bordello?"

Blair looks at the photo and shrugs. "Possibly. Maybe my grandmother knows."

I return to my changing room to undress. But the top button on the bodice won't fit back through its loop. I call for Blair's help.

She arrives in a moment. Her nimble fingers make quick work of the issue. As she helps me out of the dress, a label sewn into the back of it catches my eye. *Henrietta Hawkins*, it reads in elaborate gold lettering.

"Was this Henrietta's dress?"

"It's been in that trunk downstairs so long I never inspected it. But with that label, it must be."

I pull on my jeans, T-shirt, and sweater and step out of my dressing room as quickly as I can. "Now I'm totally weirded out," I tell Noah. "Not sure I'm ready-to-wear Henrietta's dress to a séance in her home."

He shakes his head. "It will be fine. Henrietta was a gentle soul."

"Not quite. She was a witch. *Is* a witch. A *wicked witch*," Blair says with a mischievous grin.

"How would you know?" Noah seems genuinely curious.

"Because I know her story better than anyone in town," Blair says. "Henrietta has a diary. When we were kids, Miss Lillian used to organize scavenger hunts at the library on Saturday mornings. One time, she passed out illustrations of the interior of the Salem Heritage House. We had to color it in. Then she asked us to guess where Henrietta's diary was hidden."

"You found her diary?" I ask.

"Not in physical form. But I found Henrietta—and something *very important* that had belonged to her. Since that moment, she's charged me with doing her bidding."

I can't believe what I've just heard. *The ghost of Henrietta charged a wannabe teen witch to do her bidding?*

Noah nods at Blair, the way people do when they're humoring someone who seems demented or crazy. "Would you be able to wrap the dresses up for us?" he asks.

"Sure thing." Blair moves to fold the dresses.

Suddenly, a flash of black appears at the window, just the way it did at the library earlier today. Pyewacket puts her front paws on the glass and peers in at us.

Jasper barks his most ferocious warning. Pyewacket hisses back, sending Jasper to cower under Blair's red velvet sofa. The feline slithers through the slightly open window with the grace of a queen, sleek tail held high.

"That Pyewacket," Blair says, shaking her head.

"You know her name?" I ask.

"Sure. She's a Salem landmark." Blair hands me my package. "And she was Henrietta's familiar."

"Familiar what?" I ask.

Blair rolls her eyes. "Duh. Didn't you watch *Charmed* reruns?"

I shake my head. No need to explain that I was too busy with school, helping my mom, and working at the time.

"Well, a familiar is kind of a witch's assistant."

Pyewacket pounces in front of Blair, flattening her ears to the sides of her head. She bares her sharp claws and teeth at the same time.

"Though *some cats* feel the situation is reversed," Blair adds. "We understand one another, mostly, anyway. She'll come around. In time."

"Come around to what?"

Blair sighs as she turns to me. "When you go back to New York, do yourself a favor and buy yourself a subscription to Netflix so you don't have to walk around Salem asking such dorky questions. But since you're Noah's guest, I'll explain the basics. The bond between a witch and her familiar is sacred. When one of them passes, cat or witch, the other must wait until the right partner comes along."

I shake my head slowly. "Henrietta's been dead for nearly two hundred years. Are you suggesting that Pyewacket's the same cat? That she's over two hundred years old, and has been waiting for the right partner all this time?"

"You said it, not me." Blair hands Holly her package and moves toward the front door. "Have a nice day, all."

As we exit, Blair steps out to see us off. "I'd watch out if I were you, Nina," she calls. "Henrietta wants her body back."

CHAPTER 21

The cold October air stings my cheeks as Holly and I walk toward the Salem Heritage House. As we step into the foyer, the mouthwatering aroma of fresh-baked cookies entices my appetite.

"I'm going to see if Brad needs my help in the kitchen."

Holly smiles. "Someone's *hungry*. And something tells me it's for more than cookies."

I don't blush easily, but I feel heat rise in my cheeks. "We're just friends is all. Or getting to be friends."

"Go on to your handsome chef. But bring back a bunch of cookies for me. I'm starving because we missed lunch. I'll take your dress to your room for you. C'mon, Jasp. Let's get ready for the séance."

I cross the living room and make my way into the kitchen.

Inside, Brad works from the center island, shaping cookie dough on large, steel baking sheets.

"Nina." His face lights up when he sees me. "Come

taste the best cookie of your life." He takes a warm cookie from a tray and pops it in my mouth.

I smell the cookie before I taste it, a delicious combination of sharp ginger, roasted walnuts, and what must be wine-soaked raisins.

"I've tasted nothing like this before. Chewy, and not too sweet. The texture is amazing."

"That's because the pilgrims didn't have sugar," he explains. "They used raisins for sweetness. Honey was too precious. I've made cookies from different historic recipes, but this one's my favorite." His eyes sparkle. "And I've added an herb from my garden to give it an extra hint of sweetness."

"Like that herb stevia? The stuff that comes in packets to sweeten coffee?"

An impish grin brightens Brad's features. "Yes. Something like that."

His expression reminds me of the classic Brad Collins of four years ago—the cocky, bad-boy chef who brought unique flavors together like a witch with a magical cauldron.

But back then, he purchased exotic spices from respected importers, recognized professionals with all the licenses. He didn't infuse his cuisine with experimental, homegrown herbs.

"I'm sure everyone will love these cookies tonight. I promised to take some up for Holly, if it's okay." When he nods, I place a half dozen onto a plate. "I guess the recipe Lillian found for you paid off."

"That woman is a national treasure." Brad smiles. "What did she have to say about that book you found in the study? The one with someone who looked like Moses?"

"Oh, that." I take a deep breath. Before I can respond, Brad turns back to his cookies. Yet another reminder that it's best to leave him out of all this. I look at my watch. "Shouldn't you be preparing dinner?"

Brad's face twists into a sudden scowl. "Dinner. Pinkley demanded cuisine a la Francaise. Ridiculous. He can't buy me, Nina. He may have thought he was getting a bargain when he agreed to let me work off my prison sentence here, but I'm not his slave."

Brad's outburst surprises me. "If you don't do what he requests, can't he send you back to prison?"

"He can try. We'll see how far he gets."

After a moment, Brad gently touches my cheek. "Don't worry, Nina. He'll get the fancy French cuisine he wants. I did the prep this morning after our outing." He jerks his head toward a sideboard holding containers of chopped vegetables and other ingredients.

"I could have done it in my sleep. It will all be prepared tonight, a la minute, as Pinkley requested. Moses will help me serve."

I let that sink in. "Imagine that you get out of the contract you have here. What would you do?"

"I have my eye on a place in the Hamptons." His eyes shine. "It's a small place, but right in the center of that ritzy town, Sagaponack—just the right open-minded, affluent crowd to enjoy Early American cuisine. With the right PR company, I'll strike culinary gold."

I try to meet Brad's eyes, but he's smiling, looking off into the future. Suddenly, I see his vision—a wealthy couple in designer clothes getting out of their late-model luxury car and walking up to his restaurant.

I'm surprised to see it's a reconstructed barn from a century ago—whitewashed wood on the outside, very sleek and modern on the inside. Still reading Brad's vision, I flash to the same couple seated, enjoying salads with local ingredients fresh from Brad's own farm.

"Okay, Brad." I touch his hand. "Until tonight."

Before walking upstairs to the Henrietta Suite, I glance at her portrait. Today her smile is enigmatic—not quite a smirk, but an expression that suggests she's hiding a secret.

When I open the door to our room upstairs, Jasper waddles over to greet me.

"Hi, Jasper." Putting down the cookies, I give him a quick cuddle on my way to the bedroom. I left the book with the Moses-like image on the nightstand, but now the nightstand is empty. The book's not there. I check every inch of the room, with Jasper yipping impatiently for attention as I do so.

"Holly?" I turn to her as she comes out of the bathroom. "Did you see the old book I left by my bed last night?"

"No," she says, reaching for a cookie.

"It was an important book. Do you think Moses cleans our room?"

"I made your bed and mine this morning. Why? Is something missing?"

"Just that book. I took it from Captain Hawkins' library last night."

"Well, maybe Moses came to tidy, and he put it back. Or maybe it was all a dream, and you never had the book."

"I remember sitting in Captain Hawkins' study, trying to decipher its strange lettering, before taking it back down here."

I pause. *Can it be possible that I dreamed it?* That the book doesn't exist?

Holly moves closer. "Why are we talking about some musty old book when I want to hear all about Brad's *cookies?*" She laughs, waggling her sharply arched brow.

"He's in a weird place, Holly. He's obsessed with this

Early American cuisine idea—so obsessed he's not even listening to Mr. Pinkley's requests. I'm not sure about the contract he signed, but I think Mr. Pinkley has the power to send him back to prison."

Holly lets out a long sigh. "Don't worry, Nina. Brad Collins can fend for himself. Let me help you dress for dinner."

Holly pulls out the bag with Henrietta's dress and opens it on the bed. A gossamer-fine spray of what appears to be silver glitter rises from it as she does.

"What was that?" I gasp.

"What was what?" Holly shakes out the dress, smoothing any wrinkles. The glittery spray now takes on a more solid form, like smoke.

"There are particles coming from the fabric."

Holly shrugs. "I'm not seeing it. Probably just a few centuries of dust. Let's get you dressed. I have myself and Jasper to worry about, too."

As Holly gently guides me into the dress, I understand why aristocratic ladies in former centuries needed a maid to help them with their clothes—too many buttons and bows for a woman to fasten on her own.

As Holly ties the last ribbon, a strange sensation overtakes me. I gaze into the looking glass, surprised at what I see. I walk closer, touching my image in the mirror.

"Cut it out, Nina. You're scaring me."

I hear a female voice saying something, but it's distorted and nearly inaudible, as if she's underwater. A gentle warmth permeates my body, relaxing me until I feel as if I'm floating in a soft cloud.

Still looking into the gilt-edged mirror, I realize I'm in my bedroom at the Salem Heritage House. Everything is as it was when I left—the twin canopied beds, the open windows looking out toward Salem Harbor.

But my normally pale skin has a slightly more golden glow. And though I'm wearing my favorite dress, the dress they painted me in, it hugs my body in a new way, a way pleasing to my eyes. But my beautiful auburn tresses! *Why are they falling straight past my shoulders like some commoner?*

"Curls." I speak to the woman standing to my right. She must be a new servant, though she looks vaguely familiar. I have forgotten her name. "Curls at once, or I'll be late for dinner."

The woman steps forward. She has a concerned look on her face as she speaks, but her voice is distorted. *What's wrong with her? Why can't she make herself understood?*

A small animal approaches. My heart leaps in anticipation of seeing my beloved cat. But it's a small black and white dog. His mouth is open wide, his thin lips curled up as if in a smile.

But it stops short of my extended hand.

"Come here…" As I bend forward to touch him, he whimpers and shrinks away.

Suddenly, a sharp slap stings my face.

"Nina. Nina, stop it. You're scaring me."

I wince from the pain, and my vision blurs. When it sharpens, I recognize Holly. "You slapped me? *Why?*"

"You totally spaced out. You had this weird look on your face. And you were touching the mirror. Total freak-out time. It gave me the creeps."

"I was just *looking* in the mirror."

"Yeah, but you were touching yourself—like you were making sure you were real. Then you yelled out 'Curls.' It was pretty bizarre coming from a girl who has every hair-straightening tool in the world."

"Maybe a hairstyle with curls would be appropriate for this eighteenth-century dress."

"Agreed. But you commanded me like I was your

servant or something. Then Jasper cowered away from you."

"He did?"

Holly takes a deep breath, then exhales. "It's Halloween. We're in Salem. Maybe it's to be expected. But all this talk of ghosts and witches is taking its toll on me. And you, too. It's not too late to leave, you know."

"Leave?"

"Go back to Manhattan. I'm sure we can find a train. Heck, I'll blow my life's savings on a limo, if we must. But I'm getting a weird feeling, Nina. I'm scared."

I feel scared too. But leaving would just be running away. I can't do that, and anyway, I don't want to leave Brad. Not when we're connecting so well. And I can't forget the reason I came here. I must come back with at least a major article, since it seems there won't be an advertising contract for a while.

"Let's stick it out, Holly. We just have a case of the All Hallows Eve jitters."

Reluctantly nodding her agreement, Holly uses a curling iron to replicate Henrietta's spiral curls in my hair. But despite the warmth, I feel chills.

Have I made the right decision about staying here? Would it be better to do as Holly suggests and get back to the safety of our apartment in Manhattan?

Part of me wants to shriek: *Yes, let's pack our bags and go.*

But then what about the article I'm planning on Brad's culinary resurrection? Pulling it off could ignite my career and pave the way for a better financial future for myself and my mother.

I decide to stay. *Whatever will be, will be.*

CHAPTER 22

*O*nce I'm finally dressed and coiffed, I help Holly change into her sexy bordello outfit. The blood red dress flatters Holly's voluptuous figure, and we both agree it's okay to leave her straight black hair falling to her shoulders. After all, she's a saucy brothel girl, not an aristocratic lady.

"Shall we go?" I tap my foot, eager for the night to unfold.

"In a minute. Jasper's still deciding."

"About what?"

Holly sighs. "His outfit. He can't decide if he wants to wear his Beetlejuice costume or dress as a doggy ghost."

"Ghost?" I take a closer look. "With the gold wings, he looks more like a doggy angel."

"That's because only *good* dogs go to heaven. Isn't that right, Jasp?"

We watch as Jasper circles the two costumes Holly has arranged on the floor for his inspection.

"Jasp, *choose* one," I tell him. "I like the angel ghost."

Jasper places his paw on its gold wings. Looking up at us, he yips his selection.

"Good boy, Jasp." Holly makes quick work of pulling the lightweight fabric of the costume over Jasper's back, fastening it loosely beneath his tummy. "You'll be the belle of the ball."

Jasper yips his approval as we leave the suite.

We find our group formally assembled in the living room. Moses, wearing the same eighteenth-century butler outfit as yesterday, offers guests Champagne from a silver tray.

Mr. Pinkley sits on the richly upholstered, gold-edged chair, dressed to resemble his ancestor, Captain Hawkins. His red velvet jacket and white silk shirt suit him.

"Good evening, Mr. Pinkley." Smiling, I play the role of the polite guest. "Your costume is fantastic. You look just like your ancestor."

Mr. Pinkley's dyed his graying hair jet black for the occasion to better match Hawkins' portrait.

"*Costume?* This is the real thing. I found it hanging in Captain Hawkins' closet when I first took possession of the Salem Heritage House. Didn't even need to have it dry cleaned."

I nod, smiling again. Portly Mr. Pinkley has more than a dozen pounds on his dapper ancestor, causing the buttons of the rich, golden vest to strain against their velvet loops. His navy silk trousers have a small hole in the right knee.

He stands, extending a welcoming hand. "I'm sorry we got off on the wrong foot, Ms. Brown. But you need to understand how important the Salem Heritage House is to me. When Theo Grant told me of your magazine's request for an early look, I assumed it was from Ruth Ross herself. Then I telephoned her. She assured me you're the best journalist on staff."

Ruth said that? Well, of course Ruth would build me up to a lucrative prospective client. I know only too well how quick she'll be to lash out at me for failing to get the contract.

"That was kind of her. But when will the renovations be complete? I understand there's some hesitation from the Salem Preservation Committee to approve them."

Mr. Pinkley makes a dismissive gesture with his hand. "A minor hold-up. The stroke of midnight will mark my official acquisition of the Salem Heritage House, according to the dictates of Captain Hawkins' last will and testament. Then—"

Moses appears before us. He bows to Mr. Pinkley before speaking.

"Chef Brad requests your presence, sir."

"Can't you see I'm busy?"

"He says it's urgent, sir."

Mr. Pinkley nods to Moses, then turns to me. "Well, if you'll excuse me. Temperamental chef on deck."

I feel a sinking sensation in my gut as I watch Mr. Pinkley head to the kitchen. Brad's earlier tirade against his employer put me on edge, and it seemed just a matter of time until he'd explode. But I hadn't expected it to be so soon.

Instinctively, I step toward the kitchen. Perhaps I can prevent Brad from making a scene. But before I can act, Lillian, the librarian, greets me.

She sports a colorful gypsy ensemble with a feather boa. It's hard to tell if it's a costume or simply one of her regular dresses, given her eccentric fashion sense. A vibrant red, orange, and saffron-colored scarf billows around her head, and gold rings dangle from her ears. She even has a small gold ring pierced through her hawk-like nose.

"Dear Nina, you are the absolute personification of Henrietta. Just look at you. How did you get the idea?"

"Blair found this dress for me in her vintage shop."

"Just think," Lillian says, looking me over. "It's been two hundred years since this dress was worn, likely in this very house. Do you feel any iggles?"

"What's an iggle?"

Lillian cocks her head. "I suppose most people would use the term *chills*—a feeling of déjà vu. That sensation of something being out of the ordinary."

"I do. But how did you come up with the word *iggle*?"

Lillian laughs. "My mother told me that was one of the first words I uttered when I was a toddler. We lived in an old house, you see. It brimmed over with ghosts. They were a playful lot, always trying to make me giggle. Hence the word *iggle*."

The explanation makes little sense to me. But nothing about Lillian makes much sense.

"Lillian, when I was at the vintage shop, Blair said something very disturbing as we were leaving."

"Disturbing? What was that?"

I take a deep breath. "She told me Henrietta wants her body back."

Lillian's laughing blue eyes turn serious. Her sharp intake of breath sets my heart pounding. "So it's true."

"What's true? Tell me." It takes all my self-control to resist clutching her arm.

"It's nothing to worry about, dear." Lillian flashes a weak smile. "I'm sure Blair didn't mean anything by it. Probably trying out a line she heard on some trending Netflix paranormal series. You know teens these days."

I shake my head. "You had to see the look Blair gave me when she spoke those words."

"What kind of look was it?"

"It's hard to describe. It was almost as if she was appraising me. Well, appraising my body, at least. Like she was mentally trying it on for size, seeing if it might fit."

"Fit? Fit *who*?" Lillian assumes a poker face. "Well now, if you don't mind, I'll excuse myself to get a glass of that Champagne."

As Lillian steps away and takes a sparkler from Moses's tray, I think over what I just told her. I must have sounded completely ridiculous.

Holly jostles her way toward me with a half-empty glass of Champagne. "Fun party. Too bad there aren't any hot guys here to ogle me in this badass bordello dress." She makes a swishing motion with her hips, causing the black fringe of her dress to sway.

"What do you mean? Noah's here. I saw you talking to him."

"I *love* Noah. He's a super-nice guy. But he's *Noah*. He'd like me if I was wearing a paper bag."

"What's wrong with that?"

"It's great that he likes me exactly as I am. It's comforting. But I've never dressed as a prostitute before, so I want to feel like a *bad girl* for once."

"Didn't you dress as a naughty nurse last Halloween?"

"Yes. But you'll find there's a difference between a nurse who has her moments of naughtiness and a fancy-dress hooker." Holly lifts her now empty Champagne glass in the air, winks, and goes off for a refill. Jasper follows behind her.

With a jolt of panic, I realize Mr. Pinkley still hasn't rejoined the party. I head for the kitchen to see what's going on.

I have no idea what I will do when I get there, though. *Walk in and pretend like I need a glass of water? Lame.*

Yet as I make my way through the darkened dining

room, I'm surprised to see Mr. Grant standing silently near the kitchen door. *Is he eavesdropping on them?*

Too late to back out now.

The handsome general manager looks up at me, startled by my presence. Yet he takes only a moment to recover his charm, flashing me a combination wink and smile.

Voices rise from the kitchen's interior. Then comes the sound of something large and fragile shattering on the floor.

"I'd kill you before I work here another day," Brad's deep voice intones.

It's the last thing I hear for the moment, as Mr. Grant turns to usher me out of the dining room and back to the party.

CHAPTER 23

In the relative quiet as we leave the dining room, Mr. Grant turns to me. "Did you hear that?" he asks softly.

"Hear what?" I play innocent.

"Brad threatened Mr. Pinkley's life."

"If he did, I'm sure it was just a figure of speech. He didn't mean it. Please tell me you won't do anything that would send him back to prison, Mr. Grant."

Mr. Grant looks at me, surprised. "This can't be the first time you met him?"

I shake my head. "We worked together back in LA. Yes, he's quick to anger. But he was just letting off steam."

The GM holds up his hands. "It's not for me to send him anywhere. But I've been expecting this confrontation. It's not the first time he's turned violent. I'd better call the police."

"Shouldn't we wait to see what Mr. Pinkley says? Maybe the two of them are just conducting a tense negotiation."

Mr. Grant nods, though I'm not sure he's buying it. "We'll wait for Pinkley to decide. Now let's join the others."

When I return to the foyer, the party has gained energy. Witch Wanda now holds court in the center of the room. She looks both sexy and glamorous in a tight, Morticia Addams-style dress with her athame visible in the holster around her waist.

Wanda stands close to Noah, chatting easily with him like an old friend. Holly sips Champagne and feeds hors d'oeuvres to Jasper, snuggled into a corner of the sofa.

The doorbell rings. Moses is busy serving drinks, so I follow Mr. Grant as he answers the door.

When it opens, I'm startled to see Blair Blanning standing outside, coat draped over her arm. She's dressed in an outfit I'd describe as an Egyptian goddess meets Vampira. A headband with a snake icon sits atop her long, blond hair. Around her neck rests a broad, ornamental metal collar with images of Egyptian deities on it.

Blair's sleeveless black gown is accented by elbow-length gold gloves with tassels dangling from them. In her right hand she holds a scepter, its straight shaft topped with a ram's head. It's heavy enough to be a weapon.

"Ah, Mr. Grant." Blair puts one foot through the door, like a pushy salesperson. "I'm Blair Blanning. You spoke to my grandmother about arranging outfits for your guests, Nina and Holly."

"How may I help?" Mr. Grant asks.

"I forgot to give Nina this." After giving her coat to Moses with a saucy wink, Blair digs into the bag she carries over her shoulder. She takes out a large, ancient-looking leather jewelry box.

"Nina," she says, looking up at me. "After you left, my grandmother remembered some matching jewels designed to be worn with this dress. So I spent an hour digging around in dusty old boxes, and guess what I found?" Blair lifts a necklace, bracelet, and earrings from the box. "They belonged to Henrietta herself. You must wear them tonight to complement your outfit."

Stepping closer, I recognize these as the jewels Henrietta wears in all her portraits, a combination of vivid green emeralds, blood red rubies, and golden topaz.

"Thank you, Blair. But I'm not a jewelry kind of person."

"You *must* wear it," she insists. "It's Henrietta's special night."

Witch Wanda approaches, turning to Blair with fire in her eyes. Her finger drops to touch the black hilt of her athame. "What do you mean, it's Henrietta's special night?"

Given Wanda's sharp tone, I expect Blair to back down. To my surprise, she does not.

"Just what I said. It's Henrietta's special night, Wanda. *You're not the only witch in town.*"

Wanda shoots Mr. Grant an imploring look. "Please escort this child, and her so-called jewels, out of the Salem Heritage House."

Before Mr. Grant can speak, Blair passes under his arm and into the room. She rushes over to Lillian.

From the looks of the normally composed librarian, Lillian's on her second glass of Champagne. Maybe even her third.

"Please make Mr. Grant let me stay. I've studied séances for years. I've waited for this moment. I want to see this play out."

Lillian turns to Mr. Grant. "If there's no harm in it, why not let Blair stay? Given her grandmother's delicate state of health, young Blair may well take her place on the preservation committee one day soon."

"I'm the one leading the séance, and I forbid it." Wanda all but stamps her foot.

Before Mr. Grant can comment, Mr. Pinkley strides into the room. "What's all this commotion?"

"This child insists on attending the séance." Wanda points to Blair. "Tonight's guests have all been pre-approved. Even if I could accommodate last-minute arrivals, her presence would disrupt the spirit world."

"Sorry, young lady," Mr. Pinkley says. "Wanda's in charge tonight. What she says, goes. Grant, please see her out."

Blair makes a quick gesture with her fingers at waist level. Then she murmurs something unintelligible under her breath.

Was that a spell?

Whatever Blair did, it worked. Mr. Pinkley suddenly appears as if in a trance.

"I can come in? Is that what you said, Mr. Pinkley?" Blair speaks in a high, eager, almost childish voice.

"Yes. Yes. Please, my dear, come in," Mr. Pinkley says.

"And will you ask that journalist to please wear the jewels I brought?" Blair says. "They are designed to accentuate the *power* of the dress. The outfit would not be complete without them."

Mr. Pinkley looks at me. "Please do as instructed, Ms. Brown. Grant, see that this is done."

With that, Ernest Pinkley takes Blair's hand, leading her to the room's center.

"She's dangerous, Grant," Wanda tells the general manager. "Get that girl out of here before the séance begins." She takes his arm, and they walk together to a corner of the room to continue their conversation.

A clap of thunder shatters the still air. Jasper yips his fright. I look toward the window in time to see a bolt of lightning illuminate the black Halloween sky. Already I know this will be one heck of a long evening.

CHAPTER 24

"It's past Jasper's bedtime," Holly says. "I better get him nice and snuggly under the covers."

Holly hiccups as she lifts Jasper into her arms and heads up the stairs to our suite. But minutes later, she comes back down again with Jasper swaddled in his colorful quilted doggy blanket.

"The little guy was too scared to sleep alone," she says, tucking him into a corner of the living room sofa before joining Noah.

I sit beside Jasper, stroking the warm fur of his back under his blanket. He yips softly in contentment before his eyelids flutter closed. A few minutes later, snorts and snores signal his deep, relaxed sleep.

"There you are!" Blair lunges toward me.

"Shhh. You'll wake Jasper!"

Blair glances at Jasper, shakes her head, then leads me by the hand to a comfortable chair in the foyer. Around me, the assembled guests chat with one another, almost all tipsy given the way Moses constantly refills their Champagne glasses.

"I am so glad my grandmother remembered this." Sitting next to me, Blair clasps a bracelet to my wrist, then turns her attention to a necklace she pulls from a box. "Henrietta would be so happy you're wearing her jewels."

"The two of you are on a first-name basis?" My tone is snarkier than usual, but Blair takes the comment literally.

"Oh yes. I've always felt a special alliance with her, visiting her grave and all. But now we're united in the flesh."

I don't even bother to ask what she's talking about. I don't want to know. Blair stands, then steps back to admire her work.

"May I take a picture?" she asks.

"No."

"Too late." Blair snaps a shot with her phone. "I'll be back in a jiffy."

As soon as she leaves, Holly approaches with Noah and hands me a glass of Champagne. "You need to chill out."

"I am chill." I turn to Noah. "Did you guys see the way Blair just pushed her way in here? That teen witch simply has to wiggle her nose to get people to do whatever she wants. Was she always a spoiled brat, Noah?"

"Just about. But I get where it comes from. Her sister Becca was always the best in everything. Even when she was a little kid, Blair felt she had to compete."

Noah stops speaking. He looks at me with intense curiosity. "I must admit, Nina. I didn't really see your resemblance to Henrietta when I first met you. But now, with your hair styled like hers and wearing her jewelry— man, you could be her doppelgänger."

"What's that?" Holly looks at Noah for an explanation.

"It's a German word meaning body double."

"Well, tonight, it looks like we're all body doubles for someone," Holly says, hands on hips. "Me, dressed like some eighteenth-century hooker. Noah, wearing the outfit and sword of some long-dead privateer. Ernest Pinkley dressed as Captain Hawkins. And Nina, the spitting image of Henrietta Hawkins. Halloween will never be the same."

Holly plops down on the sofa. Noah joins her. "Promise you'll hold my hand during the séance tonight."

"Of course." Noah squeezes her hand. "I'm always happy to pass the time with buxom bordello ladies. It's weird to think we're all so connected. The three of us just met, but a few hundred years ago, my cutlass, the original owner of Holly's sexy outfit, and Henrietta might have been together here in this very room."

"A prostitute in the Salem Heritage House?" My voice sounds prim, even to my ears. "How could that happen?"

"You don't know those old Salem captains." From the sound of Noah's laugh, he's had more than a few glasses of Champagne. "I've read some books in Lillian's archive. They were a lusty lot."

"*Not* Captain Hawkins." I do not know why I'm speaking so sharply in his defense. "There must have been good captains and bad captains."

"Fair enough." Noah nods. "But it depends on your definition of *good* and *bad*. How did those Salem sea-faring captains get so rich unless they did bad things?"

"Bad things like what?" The question leaps out of my mouth.

"*Wench.*" Noah's tone is playful as he turns to Holly. "Please educate your friend."

"Nina, think back to our fourth-grade history class with Mrs. Rogers. Don't you remember her telling us how the early settlers gave the Indians colorful beads for all of Manhattan? You don't know what Captain Hawkins had to do in order to become so wealthy."

Suddenly, I remember the illustration in that old book

—a white man, forcing a Jharkhand native to show him the gold mine at gunpoint.

I reluctantly nod.

Noah takes another glass of Champagne from Moses' silver tray. "Come to think of it, *wench*, since you were alive at the time, do you remember any bordello gossip about where Captain Hawkins *hid* the treasure?"

"Let me see." Holly puts her fingers to her forehead and closes her eyes. "I need to go to that space and time."

Noah gestures toward Wanda. "Hey. Maybe Witch Wanda can help us." He gets up and pulls her over. "We want to ask you a favor."

"What favor is that, Noah?"

I'm surprised by the affectionate way she speaks his name. Then I remember she's been his longtime supporter and helped him get his job with the tourism office.

"Wanda, can you make a dress talk?"

Blair, who had been speaking to Mr. Pinkley a few feet away, overhears and joins our group. "What are you guys talking about?" she asks.

Noah pats the empty place on the sofa next to him, gesturing for Blair to sit.

"The dress you found for Holly," he says. "It probably dates from the time your vintage shop was a bordello. And whoever owned the dress was probably one of its working girls. I'm asking Wanda to ask the dress if it knew a sailor who might have whispered the secret of Captain Hawkins' hidden treasure."

"Dresses do not talk," Wanda says firmly.

"*Everything* talks," says Blair. "Haven't you heard of enchanted objects, Wanda? Jeez. You can lead *old witches* to innovation, but you can't make them partake."

"Magic is not a toy." Wanda steps back. "You better

watch your step, teen witch. Little girls who play with matches get burned. *Badly burned.*"

As soon as Wanda walks away, Blair ridicules her in a singsong baby voice. *"Magic is not a toy…"*

Holly cracks up. She's had more Champagne than I thought. Even Jasper thinks so, as he shakes himself awake and taps his paw on her thigh as a signal for her to calm down.

"Hey, Noah…" Blair's tone turns serious. "I'll make Holly's dress talk for you."

"Oh, no," Noah says. "Becca would never forgive me if I encouraged her kid sister's passion for magic."

"She won't have to know. C'mon, I've always wanted to make a spirit talk."

"What's a spirit have to do with it?" Holly asks, suddenly sounding more alert. "You said you were going to make the *dress* talk."

"Yeah, I can make a dress talk, but it wouldn't have anything interesting to say. Now a person, that's another thing entirely." As Blair speaks, her eyes glow electric blue.

"What do you mean?" I gasp. Blair is totally freaking me out. "You're bringing back the dead? Isn't that what Wanda's going to do in the séance?"

"There's bringing back the dead and *bringing back the dead.* Different strokes for different folks." Blair giggles. "I like to use noninvasive magic."

"What the heck does that mean?" This girl exasperates me.

"I'll channel the *owner* of the dress to speak to us. I've seen Wanda perform in the past. Her gig is to use all those bells and whistles she learned in Las Vegas—"

"What bells and whistles?" I look at Blair. "What does any of this have to do with Las Vegas?"

"Las Vegas. Sin City. Wanda was a box jumper."

"Box jumper?" I'm only a handful of years older than Blair, but I have no idea what she's talking about.

"A box jumper is a magician's assistant," Blair explains. "They got the nickname because they scrunch themselves up in a box before the magician saws them in half. Then they release the latch on the false bottom and jump out before the dude says 'Ta-da.'"

"Are you saying Wanda's fake?"

"No." Blair laughs. "Just that *I'm* the real thing."

"I want it, Nina." Holly wiggles in her seat with Noah's arm around her. "I want to experience this magic. I want to *know* the woman who owned my dress. Tell me, Blair. Tell me everything."

"It's not for *me* to tell," Blair says. "But you must consent. You must say it. You must say, 'I agree to bring the owner of the dress into my being.' Now."

"I consent. I consent. I consent."

My heart beats wildly as I turn to my friend. "Holly. No. Earlier, you suggested we go back to Manhattan. Let's just leave. Right now."

But Holly, like Mr. Pinkley, appears to have fallen under Blair's spell.

"I want to stay." Holly's words take on a strange tone.

I turn to Blair. "What did you do to her?"

Blair smiles. "Just let the evening take its course. She'll be right as rain tomorrow. *Maybe.*"

CHAPTER 25

Restless, I decide to see how Brad's doing in the kitchen. On the way, I stop to check on Jasper. He's kicked off his blanket and lies on his back, pink tummy exposed, with his two little front paws in the air. On the opposite end of the sofa, Holly giggles with Noah.

Leaving them, I enter the kitchen. Relief washes over me as I find Brad in his classic Michelin-chef mode, holding court with an assortment of copper pots and pans. Based on the enticing aromas rising from the stovetop, the dinner he's preparing will be delicious.

I stand near the door for a moment, waiting for him to acknowledge my presence.

When he looks up, I come forward. "I need to talk to you."

"Henrietta Hawkins in the flesh." He grins, continuing his chopping. "Is the mistress of the house coming to seduce the kitchen help?"

I smile despite myself. "Not at this moment. But I would like to talk to you."

Brad stops working, concern in his eyes as they meet mine. "Is everything okay?"

Nothing is okay. But I know better than to alarm Brad when he's in the midst of meal preparation.

"I must tell you that Mr. Grant was listening to you and Mr. Pinkley arguing earlier. I was there too—it sounded serious. Did I hear you threaten to kill him?"

"I was just venting. I've made that threat before. And as of a few minutes ago, old Pinkley's still alive."

Brad's cavalier tone makes me realize Mr. Grant and I were probably overly concerned.

"Well, you should know Mr. Grant considered calling the police."

"For mouthing off at my boss?" Brad laughs. "If I were you, I'd go back and have another glass of Champagne. It's Dom Perignon Pinkley's pouring. Drink up while you can."

"You threatened Mr. Pinkley's life. Maybe you didn't mean it, but Brad, you're a convicted felon. Making a threat like that can get you into serious trouble."

"Trouble is my middle name."

"It doesn't have to be. Instead of arguing with Mr. Pinkley, why not just do what he asks? Just until your contract is finished and you're free. You can appeal that conviction and get a clean record. Then you can start up that restaurant in Sagaponack and—"

"Nina." Brad's tone is dark as he stares me down. "I don't need you to get into my business."

"Apologies. That's not why I came to speak to you."

As Brad returns to the familiar task of vegetable chopping, his mood lightens. "Okay. Speak."

"I'm not sure how you'll respond."

"Sounds serious." Brad looks at his watch. Then he twists its knob and taps its face. "I have exactly seven minutes until I get this broccoli rabe off the burner. Come to my office. I don't have a shrink's couch, though. Hope you don't mind a straight-backed chair."

I follow Brad into his office and take a seat across from him. A red tin box sits on his desk.

"A fresh batch of brownies from Wanda?"

"She makes the best," he says, breaking off a square and popping it into his mouth.

"Does this one have hallucinogens in it? When Rico took a tiny bite of the last batch, he birded out."

"Relax, Nina. It's all natural. Wanda added seeds of the wild dagga plant from South Africa. Adds a hint of sweetness and a dash of fun. Harmless. Want one?"

I shake my head. Remembering I have exactly seven minutes, I get right to it. "Something terrible is going to happen tonight."

A slow grin spreads across Brad's face. "How do you know? Are you psychic or something?"

"Yes. I've been trying to tell you, but I thought that you'd think I was crazy. But now I have no choice."

"Tell me."

I take a deep breath. "Remember, I told you about the accident that killed my father during our picnic this morning?'

"Yes."

"The doctors pronounced me dead, too. For twenty minutes. Then a nurse saw the beeps on the life support system start up again."

Meeting my eyes, Brad nods for me to continue.

"I was seven. Ever since then, I've had this ability—a psychic ability, the ability to see the dead. The first ghost I saw was my father, right there in the hospital with me. I saw other ghosts too. Then, after they released me, I could see things occur before they really happened."

Brad waits for me to continue.

"I learned to suppress it quickly, once kids at school started teasing me about it. But since the moment I came to Salem, I've been seeing ghosts everywhere. Well, certain ghosts, at any rate."

"Which ghosts are they?"

"I've seen Captain Hawkins and Henrietta."

Brad leans over the desk to take my hand. "I believe *you* believe you can see ghosts. But I've seen no ghosts here. Or anywhere. And I don't feel any strange vibes tonight."

"There's something else. I have a feeling Captain Hawkins is going to materialize tonight."

"He should," Brad says, his tone jovial. "We're celebrating the anniversary of his death, after all."

"You don't understand. Mr. Pinkley thinks he's inheriting the Salem Heritage House free and clear. But he doesn't know about the curse and—"

"A curse?" A beep sounds. Brad taps his watch. "Broccoli rabe time. Need to rescue it at that perfect moment between crisp and flaccid."

Standing, I shake my head. "I've taken enough of your time, anyway."

Brad walks me to the door, holding it open for me. "I hear these Salem seamen are a lascivious lot, dead or alive. Don't let Captain Hawkins pinch you on the way out."

At eight o'clock, a chime sounds. As the room quiets, Mr. Grant speaks. "Dinner is served." He walks toward me. "Ms. Nina, may I escort you?"

"Escort me?"

"To dinner. In the era when Captain Hawkins walked the earth, gentlemen always escorted ladies to dinner."

"In this case, a lady and her dog," I say, as a newly awake Jasper rubs his wet nose against my ankle.

Mr. Grant leads me into the dining room with its beautifully set table. Each place features a thick, cream-colored name card standing on the plate.

When we're assembled, Mr. Pinkley holds up his glass of Champagne for a toast. "Welcome, friends. Nearly two hundred years ago, my illustrious ancestor was attacked in his bed. And two hundred years ago today, he ascended to wherever sea captains go when they pass. To his spirit."

Everyone lifts their glass in salute. "*To his spirit,*" we say in unison.

"Captain James Hawkins was a great man. He sailed the seven seas in search of gold and jewels. His home, our own Salem Heritage House, was then and now as a treasure chest filled with the riches of the world."

"As his only living heir, I take formal possession of this home at midnight. The esteemed Witch Wanda Williams will invoke his spirit to give his blessing."

Beside me, Blair snickers under her breath.

When Mr. Pinkley takes his seat next to me after his toast, Moses circles the room with a silver tray. He offers each guest a portion of salmon aspic.

"Chef Collins tells me you knew each other in Los Angeles," Mr. Pinkley says to me.

"Yes. I was a server at La Toque, his restaurant there, when I attended UCLA."

"Brad Collins is a fine chef, despite his crazy ideas about pilgrim food."

"I believe he calls it Early American cuisine."

Mr. Pinkley rolls his eyes. "Clients seeking the Salem Heritage House will expect the very best French cuisine. That's what Brad Collins served at La Toque. That's why I got him out of jail to serve out his sentence here."

"Yes. He served French cuisine." I smile politely. "But he used herbal infusions to give the dishes his own interpretation. I think his idea of Early American cuisine is exciting."

"Ridiculous. No guest will pay a hundred dollars a person to munch oats. Not when they're staying in the most luxurious hotel in Salem. This masterpiece boutique hotel will—"

Wanda turns toward him. "Ernest, the house is hardly a masterpiece."

"It will be once I own it free and clear. And it would have been refurbished long ago, if your preservation committee hadn't put so many restrictions into effect."

They exchange cold, cobra-like smiles.

"Remember, Ernest…" Wanda puts her hand on his. "Tonight, the spirit of Captain Hawkins will tell us *his true wish.*"

Mr. Pinkley bristles. "His wish is written in his will. He has mandated that his surviving descendent inherit his home two hundred years to the day after his passing."

"You'll be surprised what can come out of a ghost's mouth when it speaks."

When Moses serves the second course, I attempt to make polite conversation with Miss Lillian across the table. Though she remains sitting upright and properly aims her fork into her mouth, the librarian has clearly had too much to drink.

I also keep my eye on Witch Wanda. *Why does she narrow her eyes at Holly, like she's plotting something?*

Wanda turns to Mr. Pinkley. "Will you have your man clear our plates?"

"Of course." Mr. Pinkley claps his hands. Moses emerges from the kitchen to clear the table. Holly sneaks Jasper a piece of salmon.

"Now, Holly," Wanda says. "Remember when Noah asked me to make the dress you're wearing come alive? I declined at the time. Now I think it would be quite amusing to proceed."

"Don't bother, Witch Wanda." Blair feigns a yawn. "The spell's been cast. Stop taking credit you don't deserve."

I stand. *Enough is enough.* "Holly will *not* be a part of your witch rivalry. Stop this—"

Before I can finish my words, an unseen force slams me down into my seat. *Hard.*

"Are you afraid, child?" Wanda looks deeply into Holly's eyes.

"No. Yes. No…" Holly's voice sounds strange again. Slow. *Hypnotized.*

A stab of genuine fear pierces my gut. I turn to Noah, my eyes pleading with him to stop this.

"Wanda…" Noah rises. "Maybe Holly doesn't want to—"

Before Noah can complete his sentence, Wanda flashes her black eyes at him. His hands fly to his throat, as if he's been physically attacked.

Blair mockingly claps her hands, staring daggers at Wanda. "So, the *wicked witch* still has her mojo? I bet you—"

Wanda shoots Blair a withering glance, and the girl's lips snap together as if sealed with glue. Her effort to form words results in distorted mumbles from her tightly clamped mouth.

"Such insubordination! Ernest, I will not have this girl present at my séance."

"As you say, Wanda." For the first time, Mr. Pinkley seems terrified by her display of magical power.

Wanda turns back to Holly. "Now just relax and close your eyes, Holly. What is your name?"

Holly hesitates. "I am Rhonda Baker."

"How old are you?"

"Twenty."

"Where are you? What is the year?"

"It's seventeen eighty-two. I'm working my shift. The sailors are coming in tonight. Madame wants us all to be ready."

"And who bought you the pretty red dress you're wearing?"

"My fancy man. He's going to be here soon, and Madame needs me. May I go now?"

"Go in peace." Wanda claps her hands and says something I can't quite hear under her breath.

Holly opens her eyes, jerking her head like she's shaking herself awake.

"What happened?" Holly looks at Wanda.

The witch's lips narrow into a thin smile. "The meal has ended. Now it's time we go upstairs for the séance."

Wanda signals the group to follow her. Blair, her lips still locked together, tries to rise but remains in her seat as if attached to it. As she struggles against invisible bonds, a part of me wants to help release her. But that could make an already tense situation worse.

I tap Holly's arm. "Are you okay?"

"Who is Holly?" I watch as my best friend's black eyes take in the beautiful dining room with its flickering candles. "This looks like home. Where is Madame?"

"Your name is Holly Broad. This is Jasper, your dog." I snap my fingers for The Jasp, then hold him up to her. "I'm your best friend, Nina Brown. Do you recognize us?"

Holly looks at us like we're strangers, crazy ones at that. "No."

Jasper puts a comforting paw on Holly's knee, then licks her face.

But it does no good.

"Holly." I shake her shoulders this time. *You know us. Nina and Jasper.*"

"You say your name is Nina Brown. Are you the new girl? When will the sailors arrive?"

My heart pounding with panic, I let Jasper run free and turn to Noah.

"Wanda put the spirit of that dead bordello girl in Holly's body. Let's take her to our suite. Maybe she can sleep it off."

Noah looks pale, terrified. "Necromancy spells don't work that way. Victims can't sleep them off."

"Why did Wanda pull that crazy stunt in the first place?"

"To pull rank over Blair? Who knows? Don't worry, Nina. I'm sure Wanda will reverse it. Let's get Holly up to Captain Hawkins' study. Maybe Wanda will do it before the séance."

But as we guide Holly up the stairs, a myriad of thoughts race through my mind. *What will happen if Wanda refuses to remove the spirit of Rhonda Baker from Holly's body?*

And if Wanda has enough power to raise the spirit of a dead prostitute at a dinner table, what will happen when she awakens Captain Hawkins' spirit in a formal séance?

*N*oah holds open the door to Captain Hawkins' study as I lead Holly inside. She looks wide-eyed at everything and everyone around her.

The study glistens with gold—ornate picture frames, nautical instruments, and decorative piping on burnished walnut furniture. Textured red velvet lines the walls, and precious handwoven Persian carpets cover the hardwood floors.

The only addition to the room since I last saw it is a large, round table standing in the center, surrounded by folding chairs. A crystal ball sits in the center of the table, next to a lighted candle. Wanda's taken her athame from the holster around her hips and placed it on the table.

She stands at her place, arranging her implements.

I walk up to her. "Holly's still under the influence of that dead girl. You must remove her spirit, now."

"Bookworm, I don't *have* to do anything."

"What did you call me?"

"Bookworm. That's your name, isn't it? What does Brad Collins calls you? And isn't it true that you crawled up here to Captain Hawkins' study last night, *just like a worm?* Taking books that don't belong to you is a crime, you know."

How did Wanda know what Brad calls me? How does she know I took that book? So it wasn't a dream. My eyes fly to the ceiling of Captain Hawkins' study. *Is there some sort of camera I didn't notice?*

"Having a genuine spirit in the room will be helpful for raising Captain Hawkins' ghost. Like attracts like, you know. Magical concept number one. He'll feel safer entering the earthly realm. Now, if you'll excuse me, I have a séance to perform."

When Wanda turns away from me, I approach Noah. "She won't change Holly back. We must go to the police."

"Be rational." Noah puts his hand on mine. "The police can't do anything. *It's Salem.* But don't worry. I know Wanda. She's acting like a prig now, but I'll bet you anything she'll remove that spirit from Holly as soon as the séance is over."

Together, Noah and I lead Holly to a chair in the room's corner. I'm touched by the way he helps settle her in, making sure she's comfortable.

Holly looks up at Noah, her eyes growing wide upon seeing his fancy pirate costume. "I know you. You're that naughty pirate from the ship, *Nefarious.*"

Noah indulges her fantasy. "And you're my favorite wench, Rhonda."

They giggle together.

In the opposite corner of the room, I spot Lillian sitting in a chair. She uses her feather boa to play with Pyewacket.

"Good evening, Lillian. Please excuse me. I better put Pyewacket outside now. If Mr. Pinkley sees her, no telling what he'll do. He swears she's trying to kill him."

"Wouldn't be surprised if she was," Lillian says as I

move Pyewacket to the open window. Pyewacket makes a show of rubbing her head against my hand before she scampers up a nearby tree.

"Pyewacket likes you."

"That's why I want to ask you about what Blair told me earlier." I sit facing Lillian, looking into her eyes. "Blair said that witches have an animal familiar. Typically, a cat. And that when one of them dies, the other waits for a new partner to be born. Blair was certain Pyewacket had been Henrietta's cat."

Lillian nods vigorously. "I can believe that."

I take a deep breath. *Part of me is glad Lillian's drunk. Maybe she won't remember what I tell her.*

"This morning I told you I thought Henrietta's ghost tried to contact me. Mostly with her eyes and expression. She's becoming more aggressive. Tonight, Holly said she saw my personality change as she was helping me into Henrietta's dress. She said I was saying strange things, ordering her around like she was a servant."

Lillian's eyes grow wide. "Then it's true. Henrietta wants her body back."

"Those are the *exact words* Blair said to me as I was leaving her shop. But what does it mean?"

Lillian hiccups, then raises her glass for Moses to pour more Champagne. "It means Pyewacket's your cat now."

My blood turns cold. "What are you saying?"

"I suspected as much the first time I saw you." Lillian leans toward me. "The thing is, I never thought Pyewacket would choose an *outsider*."

"Choose an outsider for what?"

"Taking Henrietta's place as her witch. You've heard the legend about Captain Hawkins' hidden treasure. But there's another: Henrietta's claim she'd return from the dead."

"But why would she return now?"

"To claim her inheritance."

"I'm not following you." *How can a little old lady drink so much?* "Henrietta is dead. Dust. She can't claim anything. Besides, in a few hours, Mr. Pinkley will be the official owner of the house."

Lillian laughs. "The inheritance is much more than the house. It's the treasure hidden within."

"What would a ghost do with a treasure?"

"When Henrietta materializes, she won't be a ghost. She'll be a person as real as you or me. Assuming Henrietta was as good of a witch as she was reported to be, it would be easy work."

"Okay. Fine." *Ask a crazy person a question, be prepared for a crazy response.* "Let's say you're right. What do *I* have to do with Henrietta wanting her body back?"

Lillian takes a sip of her Champagne. "Isn't it obvious?"

I shake my head. "No."

"She wants *your body*. To live in. To control it."

"But she can't do that." I jump up. "I won't allow it."

"I'm not so sure you have much choice in the matter. You say Henrietta took over your body for a short time when Holly helped you dress earlier tonight. Could you resist her then?"

"No. Holly said it was like I was possessed."

"There you have it. From what I've read of these things, Henrietta will take over your body slowly. She'll spend time in your everyday world, discovering your habits, learning how to keep herself under the radar. Then one day, she'll completely possess you."

"And then what?"

"That's up to Henrietta. Once she finds the treasure,

with her newfound wealth, she may become a jetsetter—
visit the most glamorous spots around the world."

"This is the most far-fetched thing I've ever heard." I
back away from the inebriated librarian.

Forget the story I'd planned about Brad and his Early
American cuisine. With all this color and craziness around
me, I could pitch the kind of article that might find the
cover of a prestigious magazine like *Vanity Fair* or *The New
Yorker*. This kooky only in-Salem story has all the larger-
than-life characters that could lend themselves to a
blockbuster film, too.

I need to write it all down quickly. Wanda's still flipping
through her leather-bound spell book. I should have just
enough time to grab my notebook from my room and
record this insanity while it's still fresh in my mind.

CHAPTER 28

Leaving Captain Hawkins' study, I avoid Henrietta's portrait as I move up the stairs to our suite. I'm surprised to find the door ajar. The flame of a burning candle glows in the room's darkness. The spice of an incense I can't quite identify tickles my nose.

Venturing toward the bedroom, I spot Blair sitting on the floor. The teen might have been banished from Wanda's séance, but she hasn't left the Salem Heritage House. From the looks of it, she's planned a ritual of her own in the Henrietta Suite. Given the trove of magical implements surrounding her, this might have been her original intent.

Blair's too involved in her spell casting activities to hear me as I enter the room. She sits cross-legged on the hardwood floor before Henrietta's portrait. The candle casts eerie shadows on the wall. It takes a moment to realize I'm seeing my own elongated, distorted shadow.

Blair recites a spell in a language I can't understand. Beyond the candle, I see a dish containing green leaves, a sharp knife, and an ancient-looking sheet of wrinkled parchment.

A doll sits across from Blair, just under Henrietta's portrait. Looking closer, I realize it's the look-alike doll from Henrietta's dresser. Next to the doll stands an oddly shaped glass bottle, likely made in the centuries before factory standardization. Inside it, I make out what looks like large iron nails resting in a yellow fluid.

Still chanting, Blair illuminates the green herbs with the candle and then blows on them to distribute their fragrance. A rustling sound fills my ears, coming from the slightly open window.

Pyewacket enters the room, her sleek body meeting the thick brocade drapes. She approaches Blair's macabre tableau with interest, her tiny pink nose twitching as it investigates the dish of green leaves.

Is that the labiatae plant? The herb Brad described as pilgrim-era catnip? Has Blair used the herb to summon Pyewacket? My heart beats wildly, realizing Pyewacket could be in danger. But I hold myself back from darting forward just yet.

Horrified, I watch as Blair uses the sharp knife to cut the fleshy pad of her forefinger. Still chanting, she drips blood onto the lips of the small doll.

When Blair raises her bloody hand toward the feline, I rush forward.

"Stop!" I snatch Pyewacket into my arms.

"*Henrietta.* You've arrived." Blair smiles at me.

"I'm not Henrietta. You've taken this too far, Blair."

"Have I?" Laughing, Blair uses the now-familiar magical gesture with her fingers to stun me.

After a brief sensation of relaxation, my shoulders slacken. Blair catches me before I fall, half-dragging me into the chair facing the mirror above the dressing table.

I open my eyes to my image, while also seeing Henrietta's reflection in her portrait. The two of us together, represented in the same rectangle of glass. Wearing identical outfits.

"Henrietta is pleased with you, Nina. She charged me to do her bidding. Now everything is as it should be for her return."

After steadying me in the chair, Blair brings the strangely shaped bottle to the dressing table.

"What's this?" I speak the words, but the voice is not my own.

"It's your very own *witch bottle*, Lady Henrietta. I dug it up near your grave in Charter Street Cemetery, just as you instructed."

When I don't respond, Blair continues. "Just think, it stood untouched for nearly two hundred years. Buried upside down, as you had commanded. Urine. Brimstone. A lock of your hair. Ten fingernail clippings. Rusted nails. Now I can bring you back to life. Give you the immortality you desire."

As Blair recites another spell, Pyewacket wriggles out of my arms. In a flash of black, she pounces on the dressing table. In one fell swoop, the cat upsets the ancient glass bottle, sending it crashing to the floor. Hissing at Blair, the cat darts out the window.

Facing me, Blair again makes those strange gestures with her fingers. But this time she looks into my eyes. "You will *remember nothing* that transpired in this room.

Once you walk out this door, you will be Nina Brown once again."

Blair takes me by the arm, half dragging me out of the suite and toward Captain Hawkins' study. At first, the hallway appears dark, shrouded in clouds. But with every step, my mental haze lightens.

"Nina, where have you been?" Noah moves toward me.

"I went back to get my notebook from our suite." I look down at my empty hands. "But I guess I forgot it. *Strange.* Is the séance starting now?"

"Soon. First, Mr. Pinkley has something to show us."

We return to the study, and a moment later, Mr. Pinkley signals for our attention. He stands just outside Captain Hawkins' bedroom.

"In honor of my ancestor, Captain James Hawkins, I've commissioned a painting I'd like to unveil now, on the two-hundredth anniversary of his murder. Please follow me into his sacred bedroom, the room where he was so brutally attacked. It is the first *public* opening of this room in two centuries."

As we stand gazing into Captain Hawkins' bedroom, I'm struck once again by its magnificent decor—its walls covered with textured, red paper, the giant bed boasting a blood red velvet spread. Everything shimmers with the exotic gold of East India plunder.

Mr. Pinkley orders Moses to stand at the side of what must be his commissioned painting, covered with a red velvet drape. At Mr. Pinkley's signal, Moses draws the velvet back with a gold-tasseled cord.

Everyone gasps.

In the painting, two men in black suits stab Captain Hawkins through the heart. Wanda strides toward the portrait for a closer look. "A rather morbid way to remember your ancestor, Ernest."

"I think he'd like it. From what I've read of him, Captain Hawkins lived for drama. That's why he set out to sail the seven seas."

As Mr. Pinkley drones on about the painting, thunder cracks in the distance. A bolt of lightning illuminates the dead Captain Hawkins in the painting.

A chill washes over me. *This is not an auspicious way to kick off the evening.*

When Mr. Pinkley finishes talking, he nods at Moses, who closes and locks the doors—our cue to gather around the table for the séance.

Moving toward my seat, I turn back to witness Moses not only locking the bedroom doors with an old-fashioned key, but wrapping an iron chain around the two handles as well. It's as if he's ensuring that whatever's inside can't get out.

But what could that be?

CHAPTER 29

"All right, everyone." Wanda clicks the gold finger cymbals she's fastened on her thumb and forefinger. The athame around her waist reflects the light above. "It's time to gather around the table now."

Moses turns down the electric lights. The paintings, artifacts, and maritime instruments in Captain Hawkins' private study gleam in the soft candlelight. The intoxicating aroma of Wanda's incense and her eerie selection of music amplify the surreal ambiance—like the screeching violins, violas, and cellos in the shower scene of the Hitchcock film *Psycho*.

Before I take my seat, my eyes fall on the portrait of Captain James Hawkins. Once again, his intense blue eyes seem to look straight at me, even following me as I move a few steps to the right. I recall that French term trompe l'œil —trick of the eye.

Yes. I'm looking at you, Nina Brown, those eyes say.

Holly, holding Jasper in her lap, sits to my left, with Noah next to her. I see that he's taken her hand underneath the table. He'll protect her.

I'm surprised to see Brad come through the main doorway. He's as handsome as ever in his sparkling clean chef's whites, Chef David's knife strapped to his side. But there's something a little off about Brad as he takes his place to my right. *Is he drunk?*

As everyone settles in, Wanda takes her sharp, sword-like athame from the holster she wears around her waist and lays it on the table.

While Wanda arranges her séance implements before her, I turn to Brad. "I'm glad you're here."

"Last-minute addition," he whispers. "Wanda insisted I attend—something about the balance of male energy."

Normally, Brad's smile warms my heart. But the way he grins at me now, with an odd, vacant look in his blue eyes, reminds me of Jack Nicholson in *The Shining*.

I shudder. There is something odd about him tonight, but it's not drink. Hoping it's my imagination, I lower my voice as I speak to him. "Now there's a newer drama," I begin, telling him that Wanda's hypnotized Holly.

"Don't worry, Nina. Wanda will reverse the spell. I'll make sure she does." But his hand is icy as he clasps mine, and his voice is hollow.

Wanda clicks her cymbals again, commanding our attention. "Tonight, the spirit of Captain Hawkins welcomes us to his private study, on this two-hundredth anniversary of his death."

Wanda lowers her head. As she recites something that sounds like a spell, goose bumps rise on my arms. Chilly air flows through the room.

"Moses will begin with a brief song of prayer to welcome our spirit guides."

A beautiful sound fills the air as Moses sings, sounding more like a musical instrument than a human. Its magical tones hypnotize me into a strange trance. I'm aware of everything around me. But it's as if everything's a dream.

"Now I call on the spirit of Captain James Hawkins. Welcome, Captain, to your very own home. We are assembled here to greet you, and to have you cast your blessing upon this house."

Wanda focuses her attention on those of us around the table. "Let us join hands now and close our eyes. Captain Hawkins, do you hear me?" she calls.

A slight breeze stirs in the room. Shadows float over my closed eyelids. Opening my eyes slightly, I peer upward. *Is that a faint swirl of wispy gray smoke above me?*

"Moses, please repeat your song of welcome." Wanda's firm voice reverberates through the room.

As Moses sings, the wisp of smoke above swirls around me like a silk scarf on a windy day. It encircles my neck and winds its way down my arms, lingering a few extra seconds at my back and waist.

I fully expect to see the smoke in front of me. But nothing. Just the flickering light from the burning candles. Suddenly, a clap of what I assume to be thunder fills the room. But the noise comes from the A-shaped wooden ceiling above, not outside the room.

"Oh, Captain Hawkins. Welcome. Welcome, my friend." Wanda's voice rings through the room. "Come before us now. Show us you are here."

We all cast our eyes up to the ceiling, then glance nervously at one another.

Something wet and slimy falls from above. I feel its viscous texture as I wipe it from my hair.

"Ectoplasm," Noah's voice calls. "Is it ectoplasm, Witch Wanda?"

Before she can answer, a thunderous noise booms from above.

"Captain James Hawkins," Wanda intones, her wet face reflecting the glow of the candle before her.

"We gather to await your presence. Two centuries ago, on this night, your life was brutally cut short. We want to acknowledge you and pay our respects."

The sound of heavy footsteps fills the air, seeming to come from all directions.

"Captain Hawkins, we can hear you now. But we would like to see you."

Something glows in the room's corner. At first, it's the shape of a small ball. But within a few seconds, it takes the form of a torso with legs. It walks toward us from the right.

Then, on the left, another orb manifests. It also transforms, this time into an upper torso, with arms, a neck, and the head of Captain Hawkins.

The two parts of his body meet near the center of the room, connecting with one another. And there I see the manifestation of Captain Hawkins. He wears the same sardonic smirk as depicted in his portrait.

"Welcome, Captain Hawkins," Wanda says.

The apparition walks around the room, examining all the things he treasured in life—his paintings, his magnificent desk, the hand-drawn maps framed on the walls.

He stops in front of Moses and extends his hand. "You've served me well these years, Moses. You and your family. I shall reward you."

Moses bends low, remaining in that position until the captain moves on.

Next, Captain Hawkins turns his attention to Wanda. "And you, witch. You are to thank for summoning me?"

"Yes, Captain Hawkins. With all due respect, I asked your permission first. And you accepted."

"And so I did."

Captain Hawkins continues to walk around the table, stopping in front of Holly. "I sense a fellow spirit at my table. How did you die, girl?"

"I was beheaded," Holly says in the high-pitched voice of Rhonda Baker. "For theft. But I didn't do it, sir. I told Judge Pinkley. But he had a grudge against me. I told Madame he mistreated me, that I didn't want to accept him again as a client. And that's when he trumped up the charge that I robbed him. But I didn't, sir. Please believe me. No one else does."

"I believe you, lass. Witch, release her. Let her rest in peace."

"As you wish, Captain Hawkins," Wanda says immediately.

I watch, transfixed, as Wanda looks directly into Holly's eyes, mutters an incantation, and makes an odd movement with her fingers.

Beside me, Holly shudders, as if coming suddenly awake. She looks around the darkened room. "Nina? Where are we?"

"It's okay, Holly." I squeeze her hand. "I'll explain later."

Captain Hawkins walks toward me. "Henrietta?" His voice is low and warm. Recognition shines in his blue eyes as he observes me wearing Henrietta's dress and jewels.

"You are *not* Henrietta," he says a moment later. "The transformation is not complete."

What transformation?

"I'm Nina Brown. We met at the train station. I'm staying in Henrietta's suite. And I—"

"Enough," he says, the crisp sound of his voice cutting through the still air. "I welcome you to my home. Know that you are here for an important reason. I'm counting on you to see it come to pass."

"What would you like me to do?"

Captain Hawkins' lips curl into an odd smile. "You will know when the time is right." When he puts his hand on my shoulder, it's not the icy touch of a ghost I would have expected. It's warm, almost like the tender caress of my father when he was alive.

Next, Captain Hawkins turns to Lillian and holds out his hand. "You are the town librarian, are you not?"

She nods. "And head of the Salem Genealogical Society. I'm so delighted to meet you, Captain Hawkins. I often talk about your life and times to the children during story hour. Now I can tell them I've met you in person."

"Praise for your good work, madame." Captain Hawkins turns to Noah. "Stand, boy."

Noah rises.

My heart beats quickly as the captain inspects him. "How dare you wear my cutlass?" he bellows. "I had mounted it on the wall in this very room."

"My parents gave it to me," Noah stammers. "They said it belonged to my ancestor."

"The name of your parents?"

"I'm the son of Meredith Baker and Joseph Samuels. I was born here. Just recently I've returned."

Captain Hawkins nods. "At ease, boy. Then the ghost rises to the ceiling, better to look down on us all.

"Among you is one who claims to be my descendant and heir. *Stand.* Don't force me to smell you out."

"It is me, Captain." Mr. Pinkley rises. "What do you wish to tell me?"

"Tonight, sir. *You shall die.*"

CHAPTER 30

With those bone-chilling words from Captain Hawkins, the flame illuminating the room extinguishes. The study fades to the deepest black I could imagine.

A moment later, the room's electric lights flicker on. I expect Witch Wanda to be a wilted mess. After all, she did just summon a spirit from the dead. But she appears amazingly fresh, her face glowing.

"Ectoplasm." Wanda rubs some of the moist, viscous liquid that dropped from the ceiling into her face. "The fountain of youth."

Holly turns to me. "What the freakin' hell was that?"

"Captain Hawkins came to life. We've just seen his ghost," I say. "And for the last hour, a ghost took over your body as well."

"Yeah. Right."

Guests rise from the table. Moses moves toward the dumbwaiter, using the pulleys to bring up Brad's Early American cookies. The room fills with their delicious fragrance.

Once he's set the cookies on a wooden buffet table, Moses offers guests more Champagne from his silver tray.

Holly accepts a glass, then flashes me a picture on her phone. "Look at this selfie I took with Noah during cocktails tonight. We're cute together, yes? The whore and the pirate."

"Very cute."

"I like Noah. Sweet. Dependable. But where is he? Have you seen him?"

"I'll go find him. After all you've been through, you need to recover."

Just as I turn away, Holly shrieks. "The doors. The bedroom doors!"

The doors vibrate like a thousand men stand on the other side, trying to break them down.

Finally, both the lock and the chains around them give way and the doors burst open.

Mr. Pinkley lies motionless on the red-velvet bedspread.

Is he dead? It's hard to tell.

This time, it's Noah's scream that pierces the air. "My cutlass."

I look up to see Noah's sword merrily dancing in the air above Mr. Pinkley's body.

Brad steps in close behind me. I feel his hand on my shoulder, but it's cold, clammy.

In the next moment, he, too, cries out. I feel the backward jerk of his body and turn to see an invisible force rip his precious knife from its holster.

"Chef David's knife. What the heck?"

Brad's kitchen knife joins Noah's cutlass in a macabre dance over Pinkley's body.

I stand, silent and astonished, as the knives dance ballet-like motions in the air.

Within moments, a third blade joins them—Wanda's athame.

Lightning flashes, followed by a crack of thunder. The light goes out, plunging the room into darkness again.

Panic wells within me as a new series of lightning bolts casts a strobe-light effect on the room. The three knives cease their dancing. They defy gravity by remaining upright as their collective tips angle downward, as if frozen in the action of preparing to pierce Mr. Pinkley's heart.

Time stands still. Then, as suddenly as the storm began, it ends.

No one speaks.

The dancing knives have disappeared.

After what must be the longest minute of my life, Mr. Grant clears his throat.

In the dark room, I make out his tall, elegant form reaching for his phone. He taps the screen.

"This is Theodore Grant," he says after a moment. "I am reporting a disturbance at the Salem Heritage House."

r. Grant's phone call to the police may have broken the silence of the room, but it hasn't quite diluted the spell of the moment. We stand fixed in our spots, as if collectively trying to sort out what just happened before our eyes.

Sirens blare in the distance.

Within minutes, the fast-paced footfall of heavy police boots race up the ancient wooden steps. The beams of their flashlights crisscross the dark room.

"Detective Smythe here," a voice calls out in the darkness. "What's happened?"

The still surprisingly calm voice of Mr. Grant explains that Mr. Pinkley's been attacked under mysterious circumstances.

Detective Smythe claps his hands for our attention. "Ladies and gentlemen, my officers will accompany you downstairs for questioning. We'll need to take your statements."

A few minutes later, the lights come back on. Mr. Grant

joins Detective Smythe in a corner of the study, presumably to fill him in on the details of the evening.

"This way, ladies." One of the young officers motions for me and Holly to follow him out of the room.

"Just a minute," I tell him. "I need to find my friend."

As the room clears of séance participants, officers and a tall, white-coated woman I presume to be the medical examiner make their way into Mr. Pinkley's bedroom. I turn as the medical examiner takes Mr. Pinkley's pulse, then lets his lifeless hand drop.

Strangely, all the dancing knives are gone.

Were they ever there in the first place?

Mr. Pinkley is pronounced dead. The medical examiner closes his eyelids, and the police photographer snaps pictures of his body from a variety of angles.

I approach Brad where he stands near the entrance to Captain Hawkins' bedroom, his face pale. He's perspiring as if he's in shock or has been drugged — possibly by those spiked brownies Witch Wanda gave him. "Are you okay, Brad?"

"That was Chef David's knife in the air." He speaks in a daze, not aware of my presence. "Someone yanked it from my holster. And then it found its way to be pointed at Ernest Pinkley's heart."

"We don't know what happened," I say. "It could have been an illusion."

But Brad doesn't hear me. His eyes, usually the vivid sapphire of the ocean, have faded as if the pigment has been sucked out of them.

"How can ghosts kill?" he murmurs. "How can ghosts even come to life?"

I put my hand on his arm. "The police are investigating. We'll find out what happened soon enough. Let's go downstairs and speak to the police."

"But my knife." Brad feels for his holster, still slung around his hips. "Chef David's knife."

Brad, typically strong and resilient, is totally losing it. Noah helps me lead him toward the staircase.

As we move past the bedroom, technicians put Mr. Pinkley in a body bag. Noah turns to me. "He's dead. *But how did he die?* You saw those knives dancing above his body. My cutlass was among them. Who grabbed it from my holster? The ghost of Captain Hawkins?"

I shake my head. "That's what someone *wants* us to believe."

"But why would Captain Hawkins kill his own kin? A living person must be behind this. Salem is in Las Vegas East. Someone skilled in the magical arts must be behind the murder."

A young police officer approaches us. "You must all go downstairs now."

I gesture to Noah to help Brad downstairs. Then I turn to the officer. "I think my friend was drugged. You'll find a red box of brownies inside the kitchen, in the chef's office. You'll want to have it analyzed."

The young police officer nods his understanding, writes something in a small book, and gestures for me to join the others downstairs.

As I enter the living area, the room buzzes as if it's intermission at some theatrical play or musical. Holly and Noah have squeezed themselves onto the small, red-velvet loveseat, holding hands. Jasper sits between them.

No one else seems distressed by Mr. Pinkley's death, or even by seeing the spirit of Captain Hawkins. No one except Brad. Seated on the sofa, he gazes straight ahead, as if replaying the evening's events in his mind.

CHAPTER 32

Salem detectives set up a contained area to conduct their interviews in an alcove off the living room. Lillian applies a coat of blood red lipstick as she waits her turn. The drama of the séance and murder has somehow invigorated her.

But she's barely sat down for her interview with Detective Smythe before he dismisses her.

Did he assume the librarian was too weak and elderly to have killed Mr. Pinkley? *Too intoxicated?* Likely he hasn't seen the heads of the wild animals she's killed in her library office.

Turning back to the interior of the room, I find Wanda sitting next to Brad on the green velvet sofa. *Is it my imagination, or did she just put her hand on his knee?*

I move closer. She definitely has her hand on his knee, and the voluptuous swell of her hip touches his—not that Brad registers any of this. He still appears in a daze.

Detective Smythe approaches them and speaks to Brad, but whatever Wanda says is enough to make the broad-shouldered detective back away.

I calm my jealousy by reminding myself that Wanda is Brad's sponsor. She's partly responsible for getting him into the prison-rehabilitation program that allows him to work off his sentence.

That's what I'll tell myself, anyway.

But why is she sending him brownies laced with some sort of hallucinogenic drug, albeit a "natural" herb?

Detective Smythe approaches me.

"Hello, detective. Are you ready to take my statement?"

"That depends on whether you have anything interesting to say."

I'm a little taken aback. "Uh, not sure I can add to what anyone else might have told you. We all saw Wanda invoke the spirit of Captain Hawkins, and the spirit told Mr. Pinkley tonight he would die."

"And so he did." Detective Smythe takes out a small black notebook.

"Do detectives still carry a pen and a notebook? Why not take notes on your phone?"

"Invariably, some lawyer would demand the phone as evidence. This is safer."

The way Detective Smythe says the word *safer* gives me the jitters. There's nothing *safe* about him. He leads me to the alcove, gesturing for me to take a seat.

"What were you expecting from this séance tonight?"

"It was my first. I'm here as a journalist. I was led to believe they wanted me to witness it because Mr. Pinkley wanted to emphasize fright tourism for the hotel."

"What is fright tourism?"

As a Salemite, shouldn't he know the phrase? "Tourism where people come to experience creepy moments from the past."

He nods. "And?"

"Documenting ghosts will attract more visitors to the Salem Heritage House, tourists interested in fright-based experiences. They wanted me to write about the séance in my article."

"Do you believe the ghost of Captain Hawkins really appeared?"

"I'm not sure. When I first saw Wanda invoke the spirit of Captain Hawkins, I thought it could have been some sort of light trick, an illusion—the kind they have in Las Vegas and other places, performed with smoke and mirrors. Then, after the séance, I saw the swords dance over Mr. Pinkley's body—"

"Tell me about the sword dance."

"We were all chatting in the study, nibbling on cookies. We heard the doors of Captain Hawkins' bedroom rattling. Then we heard a scream. The doors burst open of their own accord."

"Continue."

"Three sword-like objects appeared out of nowhere and danced in the air. At least, it seemed like they came out of nowhere. I recognized Brad's chef knife right away. Then I saw Noah's cutlass—he had been wearing it around Salem earlier on our walking tour. It took me a few moments to recognize Wanda's athame. The witch's knife she wears in a holster around her waist."

Detective Smythe jots something down. Then he looks up at me. "How did it end?"

"The sword dance stopped with the points of all three weapons pointed at Pinkley's heart. The weapons just floated there, defying gravity. Then the room went black."

Detective Smythe puts down his pen. "Did any of the swords penetrate his heart?"

I shake my head. "It didn't seem so, but I guess I can't be sure. It seemed like he was already dead."

Detective Smythe stands. "We'll be in touch."

"Do you know who killed Mr. Pinkley?

"That's what I'm going to find out."

After Detective Smythe leaves, Mr. Grant comes toward me with a cup of tea. "How are you holding up?"

"Better than I thought."

"An unfortunate way to end your visit with us. I'll arrange for a driver to take you and Holly to your train tomorrow."

"What will happen to the Salem Heritage House now that Mr. Pinkley's no longer with us?"

"That remains to be seen. But as Ernest Pinkley had no heirs, ownership of the Salem Heritage House will revert to the Salem Preservation Committee."

"What about your job as a general manager?"

"I took on the title of GM for this interim period, but I'm really the founder of my own operation, Unique Hideaway Resorts. We find historic or otherwise unique structures and turn them into luxury hotels."

"Sounds like an interesting business. Do you finance the hotels? Or do they pay you something like a management fee?"

Mr. Grant flashes a movie-star grin. "Ah, journalists. I love their curiosity. You'll find there are many ways to structure the deal."

"If this place falls under the stewardship of the preservation committee, what will they do with it?"

Mr. Grant shrugs. "Well, it's up to them, of course. Given their need for funds, they might commercialize it."

"Like charge money for tours?"

"That or complete Pinkley's vision of turning it into a hotel and reap the profit. But it's too early to say, Nina."

"And Moses?"

"That's also for the preservation committee to decide. He'll likely resume his previous duties under Captain

Hawkins' will. Sleep well, Nina. I'll see you tomorrow before you leave."

As I enter the foyer, I'm surprised to see Moses and Brad clearing dirty plates from the coffee table. Holly's slumped over on the sofa, snoring gently with Jasper snuggled in her arms. Noah sits nearby, watching over them.

"The Henrietta Suite is just up the stairs," I tell him. "If you don't mind helping them up to bed, that would be great. I need to talk to Brad for a moment, and I'll be right up."

"Sure thing."

Noah wakens Jasper, then Holly. As he leads them up the stairs, I make eye contact with Henrietta's portrait.

This is the first time she's seen me wearing her clothes, her jewels, and my hair in the style she wears in her portrait.

At first, her expression shows no change. Then, in agonizing slow motion, I see a dot appear on her forehead. The dot changes shape, transforming into a small letter z. *Just like my scar.*

I'm so startled, I don't even hear Wanda come up behind me. She takes my arm, her long, red nails scraping against my skin like talons. "Ms. Brown," she hisses, her voice so low it's barely a whisper.

"Unless you'd like me to summon a spirit to penetrate *your soul,* I suggest you stay as far away from Salem as possible. Your friend Holly was lucky Captain Hawkins intervened. I could have easily forgotten to remove that pesky prostitute spirit from her being."

"Why did you do it, Wanda? Why Holly?"

"To teach *you* a lesson. To show you my power. What were you trying to find in Captain Hawkins' library, Nina? *Why did you take that book?*"

I shake myself out of her grasp and move to the kitchen, expecting to find Brad. But Moses alone loads plates into the dishwasher.

"Oh," I say, surprised. "I was hoping to find Brad."

"He went to bed, Miss. Severe headache."

"Then allow me to help you." I grab a few saucers and put them in the dishwasher. "

Chef Brad speaks highly of you. I'm concerned about him. Have you ever seen him like this?"

Moses' solemn face never changes expression as he nods. "Yes. A few times. He falls into these moods. I call them spells."

"Spells?"

"In my ancestral country, when someone looks that way, we say an evil jinn's taken over his spirit."

"Brad's under attack by a jinn? I'm not sure I know what a jinn is."

"Dark witchcraft."

My skin crawls as I hear these words. Moses' image in the book I took from the library comes to mind. Then I remember what Lillian said about Moses.

Does he come from a family of Jharkhand witches? I shudder, remembering the horrific images of demons torturing and feeding upon their victim.

"Is that what happened here tonight?" I look Moses in the eye. "Was it dark witchcraft?"

"It is not for me to say, Miss Nina. But I will tell you something. You must promise not to tell the police."

"Why can't I tell the police?"

"Because her magic is powerful. Too powerful."

"Witch Wanda. Just as I thought."

"Wanda?" An amazed expression crosses Moses' face. "Miss Wanda and Ernest Pinkley were the best of friends. The lady is distraught, madame. Didn't you see her reaction when she saw Mr. Pinkley dead? Didn't you hear her scream?"

"I just figured that was good acting."

Moses looks into my eyes. "When I first met you, I understood you to have the gift."

"Gift? What do you mean?"

"You've seen her, haven't you?"

"Seen *who*, Moses?"

His voice is a whisper. "Henrietta."

"You've seen her too?"

Moses opens his eyes wide. "I always suspected Henrietta's portrait was a temporary prison. The moment you entered the Salem Heritage House, her spirit emerged from her portrait like a butterfly. And the night of the séance, I saw her fly inside of you."

"Fly inside me?" His words terrify me. "How can you see this, Moses?"

"I have the second sight. I've always been able to see that which is invisible to others. Blair Blanning uses powerful witchcraft," he continues. "Dark witchcraft. Dangerous witchcraft. She is helping Henrietta take over your body."

So Lillian wasn't drunk when she said the same thing. Revulsion vibrates through me. "Is Henrietta inside me? Inside me *now*?"

"She is inside you, yes. But Blair is a new witch. Young. Inexperienced. Her power is not strong enough to summon the energy to make Henrietta's transformation happen all at once."

Moses turns to leave.

"Wait. You can't just leave me like this. If Blair is using magic to help Henrietta enter my body, is she the one who killed Mr. Pinkley too?"

"This is for you to find out."

CHAPTER 33

Morning light filters into the Henrietta Suite. The clock reads 8 am. Everything that happened last night seems like a dream. On the twin bed across from mine, Holly stirs.

"What's that light?" Holly removes a pink satin eye mask from her sleep-puffy face. "Is it morning yet?"

"Yes. I suggest we pack up and get an early start."

"Do you think they'll have breakfast for us, considering all that happened?"

"I'm already smelling the coffee, I say, wondering if Brad's the one who made it.

"Okay." Holly gets out of bed and rummages around in her suitcase. "Jasper must be starving. I better give him a snackeroo to tide him over."

"Break the snack in half, Holly. The veterinarian said he's a few pounds over his ideal weight."

"Aren't we all?" Holly tears open a yellow canine snack pack with her teeth. Shaking out a miniature dog bone, she offers it to our hungry pooch.

"Salem was a nice idea. But can we visit one of those

luxury doggy spas for your next article? I can see it now: Jasper and me lounging in a fancy cabana. Maybe getting one of those outdoor massages in front of a blue ocean."

Jasper yips in excitement. He and Holly turn to me with shining eyes.

"Don't get your hopes up. The gravy train may end soon."

"What do you mean?"

"I promised Ruth I'd come back with a fat contract for a year's worth of advertising. The hotel is nowhere near ready to advertise, and now the boss is dead. Seems like any potential contract is off."

Holly strokes Jasper's plump tummy, a puzzled expression on her face. "What does *that* have to do with our luxury doggy spa vacation?"

"It means I may be out of a job."

"She's not going to fire you for that. It's not like *you* murdered Ernest Pinkley."

I shake my head. "You don't know Ruth Ross. Even if she doesn't fire me, she'll make me feel ridiculous until I quit."

Holly points at me. "You have a Plan B. I know you do. For your next assignment, just find a place with no witches, ghosts, or century-old curses, please."

"Got it. I'm going to take a quick shower before breakfast."

Hearing his favorite word, *breakfast*, Jasper waddles toward the portable wardrobe Holly set up for him. Using the moist tip of his nose, he sorts through his doggy outfits. A fluffy white robe captures his attention. He swipes at it with the nails of his right paw, signaling his choice.

"Looks like a certain someone wants to go down to his last Salem Heritage House breakfast in style," says Holly.

Fifteen minutes later, the three of us walk down the

staircase. As I approach the first floor, I'm almost afraid to look at the portrait of Henrietta.

Under normal circumstances, it would be easy to dismiss Lillian and Moses as wild-eyed eccentrics. Whoever heard of a departed soul living within the pigment of an oil painting?

But how else can I account for the things no one could explain? Like Wanda channeling the spirit of a long-dead prostitute into Holly's body? Or the way Holly claimed I'd been temporarily possessed by Henrietta's spirit?

Mr. Grant greets us at the entrance to the dining room. Despite the murder just hours earlier, he looks rested. As usual, he wears an expensive-looking, well-fitting suit. I greet him with a bright smile but wish Brad was here for the breakfast duties.

"Ladies, good morning. And hello, Mr. Jasper. May I commend you on your sense of style, sir."

Jasper responds with a polite yip. His white doggy bathrobe boasts a gold insignia. White slippers snuggle his four paws, keeping them toasty warm in the morning chill.

Mr. Grant gestures for us to sit down at a table he's set with fruit, yogurt, and delicious-smelling warm croissants. "What may I bring you to drink?"

"Coffee, coffee, coffee, pretty please." Holly makes a praying gesture with her hands.

"Tea for me, thanks," I say as Moses walks into the room. Mr. Grant nods toward Moses to fulfill our requests. I notice once again how he moves with a tall, straight back.

Mr. Grant moves to the sideboard, returning with a gleaming pewter bowl in his hand and a starched white napkin resting over his forearm. He resembles a high-end sommelier in a fancy restaurant. "Would Mr. Jasper prefer flat or sparkling water?"

"Flat's fine," Holly says.

"*Alakazam.*" From behind his back, Mr. Grant takes out a bottle and pours Evian into the bowl.

Jasper laps it up.

Holly claps her hands in delight. "Mr. Grant, you really love dogs. Have you ever had one of your own?

The suave general manager shakes his head. "Never lived in one place long enough to settle down," he says, going back to the kitchen.

"I bet he was a stage actor," says Holly, taking a sip of coffee. "He has this presence about him. It's more than the way he dresses and talks."

"Maybe." I watch as Holly digs her photo-printing equipment from her bag. She taps her device, and a half-dozen color photos pop out of her miniature Bluetooth printer.

"You took pictures during the séance?"

"My camera's always working."

"Let me see."

I quickly flip through her printed-out photos. "You've captured the events surrounding the murder, Holly. Some of them, anyway. Look—here's where we all gathered after we heard the scream. And this photo. It looks almost black. It must have been the dancing swords."

Mr. Grant returns from the kitchen.

"Mind if I look, ladies?" He inspects the printed photos. "You certainly caught some interesting details, Holly."

"Hey, there's Noah's cutlass." I point at the tip of the weapon jutting out from under Mr. Pinkley's bed. "I didn't see any of the weapons with my own eyes. Interesting that your camera found it."

"That doesn't mean that Noah's involved, does it?" Holly twists her fingers together.

Mr. Grant looks down at the photos. "These photos may contain important evidence."

"Against Noah?" Holly looks up at him.

"Against the person who killed Earnest Pinkley. We must get them to the police."

Holly shakes her head. "I don't want to do that."

"If the police find out you're withholding evidence, they can accuse you of obstructing justice. You may have to do jail time. You don't want that, do you?"

"No."

"Well then, just give them to me, and I'll get them over to Detective Smythe. I've booked your train tickets. A driver will take you to the station at three this afternoon."

Holly reluctantly gives Mr. Grant the photos. We glumly finish our breakfast and head back up to our room.

As soon as we're inside, Holly throws herself on the bed.

"I should never have brought those photos downstairs to breakfast. Do you think I got Noah in trouble, Nina?"

"No. Can you imagine Noah hurting anyone? And he'd never stain his precious cutlass with blood."

We both laugh.

"You better call him, though," I tell her. "Tell him the police have pictures of his cutlass near Mr. Pinkley's body."

Holly reaches for her phone but pauses before she makes the call. "It's better if we give him the news in person."

"Okay. Ask where we can meet him."

As Holly makes her call, I think back over the photos I saw on the breakfast table. And what about the ones I didn't see? *Who else among the séance participants may be a suspect?*

CHAPTER 34

J follow the directions on my phone to walk the short distance from the Salem Heritage House to the Charter Street Cemetery, where we've agreed to meet Noah.

As we pass the Peabody Essex Museum, the abstract, modern structure looks out of place with Old Salem's red-brick buildings. I unfurl my compact black umbrella, sharing it with Holly, as the rain falls harder.

Holly points to an advertisement for the museum's current exhibition. The sign reads: The Witch Bottle: *Protection From Evil?*

"Look, Nina, that's the exhibition I saw advertised on Essex Street that first night. Can we pop in?"

"Maybe, if we have time. The cemetery is over there." I look up from the map on my phone. "That wooden structure is called the Welcome Center. It says here it was originally a house belonging to Samuel Pickman, built in 1665."

"Who's Samuel Pickman?"

"No idea. But I guess we'll find out soon enough."

A few moments later, we step into the refurbished wooden building, transformed to a combination gift shop and ticket counter. They crammed every square inch with souvenirs—miniature gravestones, baseball caps, jewelry, and brightly colored toys.

One table overflows with oddly shaped glass bottles. *Witch bottles*, the sign reads. They're souvenirs folks can buy after touring the exhibit.

Lifting one into the light, I see rusted iron nails inside, and what looks like a lock of hair. A strange, dizzy feeling overtakes me. *Why does this strange bottle look familiar?*

"May I help you ladies?" A friendly woman with bright blue eyes comes toward us.

"Yes," I say. "What is a witch bottle?"

"It's a magical tool." The saleswoman seems delighted that I asked. "In Salem's early days, making a witch bottle was a way common people protected themselves from malicious witchcraft and sorcery. And…" The woman looks around to make sure no one overhears. "A way a witch could ensure she could safely return in another time, after her death. Typically, she ordered that it be buried near her grave."

"Are witches buried in Charter Cross Cemetery?"

"They could bury here no witch, since it was sacred ground back then. But that's not to say there aren't *secret witches* lying here. Recently, local news headlines claimed someone had broken in to dig up a historic relic."

The woman lowers her voice. "Supposedly, he may have escaped with a genuine witch's bottle."

"This witch's bottle thing is not as exciting as I thought." Holly tugs at my coat sleeve like a child. "C'mon, Nina, we're late meeting Noah." Holly turns to the saleslady. "We're meeting a friend. Can you show us to the cemetery?"

"Just this way."

When we step outside, the cemetery looks especially mysterious, with low-hanging fog thick enough to obscure the eerie stone markers.

We spot Noah sitting on a green-painted iron bench. His phone and a portable tripod rest beside him.

Noah's face lights up as we approach. I dread telling him the news about his cutlass.

"Nice to see you, ladies." He jumps up to kiss us both on the cheek. "You look remarkably refreshed, given what's happened."

"We slept well because of exhaustion," I say. "The weird thing is that last night didn't seem like we witnessed a murder. It was more like a theatrical performance. Until the police arrived, I almost expected Mr. Pinkley to get up and take a bow."

Noah sighs. "Me too." But after a moment, he brightens. "Hey, where's The Jasp?"

"He wanted to dress up special for you." Holly reaches into her bag. "Close your eyes."

"Okay, they're closed."

Holly gently places Jasper on the wet cemetery ground, sprinkled with recently fallen leaves.

"Oh man, Holly." I groan when I get an eyeful of what Jasper is wearing. "You didn't."

But there stands Jasper, proudly wearing Holly's newest creation: a lightweight doggy skeleton outfit.

"Jasp, my man." Noah lifts our pooch high in the air. Then he whirls him around so the skeleton-print fabric flies like a magic cape. "How's it going, Mr. Bones?"

Jasper yips happily.

"I hope this isn't disrespectful to the dead." Holly glances nervously at the cemetery's many gravestones. "But

I couldn't think of a more appropriate place for Jasper to wear it."

"The question is, why did you make the outfit in the first place?" I ask. "Rather morbid, isn't it?"

"I thought so when a client asked me to custom-make it as a Halloween outfit. But then his friends wanted the same outfit for their own dogs."

I raise my eyebrows and look at Noah. "It has to be some new East Village trend in Manhattan."

"Noah," says Holly. "Since we're here at the cemetery, would it be okay if I shoot a few pictures of Jasper modeling this outfit for the winter catalog?"

"Sure. Would you guys like a brief tour of the place first? I come here every Sunday."

"You spend Sundays in the graveyard?" I ask.

"I like to film videos here. Every week, I talk about a historical figure buried here. Everyone loves it."

"Cool." Holly looks down at a gravestone near her feet and reads the name. "*John Hawthorne*. Who is he?"

"Is he related to Nathaniel Hawthorne?" I ask. "The man who wrote *The House of Seven Gables?*"

"What's a gable?" Holly looks from me to Noah.

"Have you seen parts of houses that look A-shaped at the top? That's a gable. Nathaniel Hawthorne wrote a gossipy book about a local house here in Salem with seven of them. John Hawthorne was the writer's great-great-grandfather. But before I geek out on Salem history, what's the big news you ladies wanted to tell me?"

Holly and I look at one another. I clear my throat. "Remember last night you freaked out about your missing cutlass? Well, Holly printed out the photos she took last night, and we spotted it in one picture. The good news is that it's not missing. The sort of bad news is that Mr. Grant insisted on giving the photos to the police."

"Why?"

"He told Holly that if she didn't give the pictures to the detectives, she could be charged with concealing evidence."

"But finding my cutlass near Mr. Pinkley's body doesn't mean I killed him."

"We're sure you didn't kill him," I say. "But having your cutlass in the picture complicates things. We can sort it all out. Let's start with the basic question every detective will ask: Did you have any reason to kill Mr. Pinkley?"

Noah looks up at me, a defiant look in his eyes. "Yes."

"What?!"

"But if you ask around, I bet everyone had a reason to kill Mr. Pinkley," Noah adds.

"What is your reason?" I'm not sure I want the answer.

"Remember, I told you a card shark cheated my mom out of her family's candy shop?"

I shake my head. "I don't remember you using the word *cheat*. You said your dad *lost* it gambling with a card shark."

"Ernest Pinkley was that shark. Pinkley was young back then. He'd gone out to Las Vegas after high school to take one of those casino jobs. Then he came out here and worked at private gambling parties. My dad was a gambler, a bad one. And that's how he lost the shop to Pinkley."

"That happened when you were a kid. If it's true, why did you wait over fifteen years to kill him?" Holly asks.

Noah shakes his head. "I never said I killed him. I said I had a *reason* to kill him."

I open my mouth to ask another question, but suddenly I lose my train of thought. The strange, diaphanous mist in the cemetery thickens into a viscous fog.

Holly and Noah move closer to me. I see their mouths working. But their words are too distorted to understand. Behind them, a woman glides toward me in a dreamlike fashion. As she gets closer, I recognize her dress and clear blue eyes.

Henrietta Hawkins.

"Watch out," she whispers through the swirling gray mist. "I'm coming for you."

CHAPTER 35

"Nina. Are you okay?"

I hear a voice, distant and distorted.

"You're scaring me. Nina, look at me."

I blink, and after a moment, I recognize Holly. "Why are you shaking me?"

"You totally lost it—just like you did last night before the séance. You went completely blank. What happened? Where were you?"

I try to remember. "I saw mist. Then thick fog. In my mind's eye, the image of Henrietta floated toward me."

"Noah, is Henrietta Hawkins buried here?" Holly asks.

He nods. "Yes. Captain Hawkins too."

"Noah, as we were leaving Blair's shop, do you remember what she said to me?" I ask.

"No."

"She said 'Henrietta wants her body back.'"

"Blair's always saying off-the-wall things."

"Ever since I arrived at the Salem Heritage House, I've felt like Henrietta was reaching out to me. When I told

Lillian, she agreed Henrietta could be trying to claim my body. Moses suggested the same thing."

Holly's eyes go wide. "You spoke with Moses? Alone? I'm surprised he didn't reach into your chest and pull out your heart. That guy terrifies me. Seriously."

"Ladies." Noah holds up his hands like a referee. "Salem 101. Take anything Lillian the librarian says with a grain of salt, especially when she's been drinking good Champagne."

"Holly believes me, don't you, Holly? Last night, you said I threw a hissy fit and demanded you curl my hair. That's not like me, right?"

"The last thing you'd *ever* ask is for your hair to be curled. Agreement there."

"And recently, some things look familiar. But I don't have a real memory of them—like those witch bottles on display in the gift shop. It's like I saw them in a dream or something."

"Nina, the stress of the weekend is getting to you. It's getting to me, too. This afternoon, we'll be on a train back to New York. Until then, let's make the best of it. Why don't you rest on that bench while Noah helps me with Jasper's photoshoot?"

I sit while Noah and Holly prepare Jasper for the photos. Holly tears open a pet-safe wet wipe and cleans Jasper's eyes, nose, and paws. Then she grasps him firmly, brushing his coat until it shines.

Unlike the prima-donna human models I've read about in magazines like *Vogue*, Jasper waits patiently for his moment before the camera. As soon as he hears the shutter click, he goes into full-blown supermodel mode. His playful antics during the photo shoot lighten my mood.

"I'm hungry," Noah says once they've finished. "You ladies want to go to brunch? I know just the place."

It's a short walk to Red's, which Noah says is the most popular Sunday brunch spot in town.

"This is about as classic old-school Salem as you can get, right?" he says when we arrive. True to its name, they painted the restaurant red with white doorframes.

"This is too cool." Holly gushes. "What a great backdrop for Jasper to model his dog out-on-the-town outfit."

Hearing his name in connection with the word *model*, Jasper leaps from Holly's bag.

I sigh. "Holly, don't you have enough pictures yet?"

"There's no such thing."

Settling herself on a nearby bench, Holly unwraps two items of clothing she had stored in her doggy bag. "Which one, Jasp?"

In her right hand, Holly holds a simple white collar with an attached sky-blue tie. In her other hand she holds a red child's bib with the words *brunch, please* printed in yellow.

Jasper swipes at the bib, tearing it from Holly's hand in a single motion.

"The Jasp has spoken." Holly fastens the bib loosely around his neck. "Good choice, given the way this adorable slob eats."

Noah and I watch as Holly places Jasper on a windowsill outside of Red's. An expert in his trade, Jasper knows just how to angle his head as Holly snaps away.

When she's finished, we finally enter the establishment.

Noah greets the hostess affectionately. "It's four of us today."

"Where's the fourth in the party?" she asks.

"Right here." Holly scoops Jasper up, animating his right hand so he waves at the hostess.

"Ah, I see. Well, follow me Noah, ladies, and…dog."

The restaurant hums with activity. Servers dart back and forth, fetching guests coffee and pancakes so huge they spill over the edges of the plates.

Before we sit, Noah turns to Holly. "Does Jasper need one of those baby things?"

"Like a highchair? No need," she says. "We'll position him right between us, Noah, on your end of the banquette."

I wait while Holly settles herself in, and Jasper sits upright between her and Noah. He rests his two front paws on the table in anticipation of a good meal.

"Take a picture of us with my camera, Nina. For the scrapbook."

Recognizing the word *picture*, Jasper sits up straight and favors the camera with his open-mouthed, I'm-having-a-good-time doggy grin.

With picture-taking finally out of the way, Holly leans close to Noah. "This restaurant looks so charming. What's its history?"

"Just a local spot popular since the sixties. But the building itself dates from 1608."

"Was it called Red's Sandwich Shop back then?" Holly feeds Jasper a treat from her bag.

"It was called the London Coffee House, yet famous for its hot chocolate."

Holly looks at him, impressed. "How do you know?"

"Lillian showed me a sketch from the library's private collection. It was like the Starbucks of today. All the cool people in town came here to hang out."

I meet Noah's eyes above my shiny plastic menu. "Is Lillian a good friend of yours?"

"*Friend* isn't the right word. I've known her since I was a kid. We've become closer since I moved back to Salem. She's helping me trace my family's genealogy. My mom's folks are old-time Salemites—goes back to the witch trials, from what I've heard."

"Have you found any skeletons in your family closet?" Holly asks.

"Not too many skeletons to be had. From what Lillian and I can see, I'm the last man standing."

Noah's tone reflects a touch of sadness. He seems vulnerable. I envision him as a small child, sad and lonely —wishing for a sibling. Then later, perhaps blaming himself for his father's desertion.

"What should we order?" I ask, trying to lighten the mood. "The lobster omelet with home fries or one of those enormous pancakes that look like flying saucers? On second thought, maybe the blueberry French toast."

"Let's all order something different and share," Holly suggests. "Nina, you choose."

"Oh no. Give Noah that honor. He doesn't have to sleep next to you when you gripe at me for ordering the wrong thing."

Noah calls the server over. We're all delighted once Noah orders, and the server returns quickly with our food. Besides Holly's choice, Noah ordered an "all-meat" omelet, which takes up the entire plate. From what I can tell, it's stuffed with bacon, ham, steak, sausage, kielbasa, and American cheese.

"Now that's what I call an omelet." Holly stabs it with her fork. "Can I give The Jasp a piece of the bacon? It's his favorite part."

Noah nods.

"Will you come visit us for Thanksgiving?" Holly asks, grabbing a thick-cut French fry and dipping it in ketchup. "Nina's mom makes a mean turkey."

"Your mom cooks?" Noah smiles at me. "It's been a while since I've had a home-cooked meal."

"Making turkey was always her thing when I was a kid. These days, we have Thanksgiving dinner with my Uncle Snicker, Aunt Rose, and the twins."

"Uncle Snicker?" Noah laughs. "That's his real name?"

"Nina named him that when she was a kid." Holly thumbs in my direction. "Because he's always laughing at weird things."

"Your dad's not in the picture?" Noah looks at me.

"Nope."

We're silent a moment, and then Holly turns the conversation back to food. "This lobster omelet is the best."

We all stick forks in one another's food until there's nothing left on any of the plates.

Noah's about to pay the check when I sense someone approaching from behind us. Turning, I see Detective Smythe.

"Noah Samuels, please rise," he says.

"What's up, Detective Smythe?"

"I'm sorry, but I need you to accompany me to the station."

"Why?"

"You're a person of interest in the investigation of Ernest Pinkley's murder.

CHAPTER 36

It's a quick walk from Red's Sandwich shop to the Salem Heritage House. As we enter, Moses walks down the staircase carrying a heavy-looking box.

"I've packed some of Mr. Pinkley's belongings," he says to Mr. Grant. "Where shall I place this?"

"Right here, near the door. Thank you." Mr. Grant turns back to us with a smile. "Did you enjoy your morning, ladies?"

"We had brunch with Noah Samuels," I say. "But as we were finishing, Detective Smythe took him in for questioning. What would Noah have to gain by killing Mr. Pinkley?"

"That's what the police are trying to determine, *officially*," says Mr. Grant.

I tilt my head. "What do you mean by *officially*?"

"It's an open secret that Noah resents Mr. Pinkley for taking his family's candy shop."

"Open secret? That happened years ago when he was a kid."

Mr. Grant shrugs. "Resentment like that can last a

lifetime. Just last week I overheard him drunk, in a local bar, swearing to get revenge."

"Noah? Drunk? Swearing?" Holly shakes her head dismissively. "Doesn't sound like the Noah I know."

Mr. Grant removes his phone from his jacket pocket. He taps it a few times. And shows us the screen.

Sure enough, there's Noah in a grainy video on a local gossip website. He slurs his words as he rants against Mr. Pinkley.

"This video hit the Internet this morning. I'm sorry I had to show it to you."

Holly appears visibly shaken. I take her hand.

"Are you ladies packed up?" Mr. Grant asks. "I can order the car to come around right now, if you wish."

"No, I haven't finished yet. I'd also like to say goodbye to Chef Brad. Where is his room?"

Mr. Grant hesitates. "You'll see a door just off the kitchen."

I stand in front of Brad's door a full minute before I summon the courage to knock. "It's Nina. I've come to say goodbye."

After a moment of shuffling noises, the large wooden door opens. "Come in," Brad says. "The room's not much. But better than a prison cell."

As I enter, I inhale Brad's strong, male aroma— perspiration and a salty, spicy element I can't quite identify.

His room is not as large as the Henrietta Suite, but it's a good size for a bedroom. The wood flooring looks every bit of its two-hundred years old beneath the veneer of polish. The brightly patterned Oriental rug gives the sitting area classic elegance.

Brad gestures for me to sit in one of the two stark wooden chairs as he opens the window wide to let in some fresh air. Rico stands on a branch within his aviary. When he sees me in Brad's room, he hops onto a closer branch and sings the classic Rick James song.

"Give it to me, baby," he croaks. "Give it to me, baby."

I blush.

Brad is quick to close the window. "The fresh Salem air does you good, Nina."

Heat rises to my cheeks as I delight in the compliment. But I can't return it. Today Brad looks far from stunning with his bed-tousled hair and wrinkled, white-cotton pajama bottoms. His typically vivid blue eyes appear faded.

"They've taken Noah in for questioning, "I tell him. "You might as well prepare yourself. You could be next."

"I'm not sure what I can tell them they don't already know. The thing is, I can't remember much at all. You were in the kitchen. I was focused on getting that broccoli rabe out of the boiling water while it was still crisp. I remember sending Moses into the dining room with the entrée. Then the rest is a blur."

"Have you considered that Wanda might have drugged you?"

"What do you mean?"

"Those brownies. We both saw how they affected Rico. And he's a tough old bird."

Brad doesn't laugh. "That's crazy, Nina. Wanda's my friend. Why would she drug me?"

I take a seat. "Maybe she was trying to set you up as the fall guy for Pinkley's murder."

"Why would she want him dead? They've been friends since high school—even before then. And until the preservation committee clamped down on renovations, he was her biggest political supporter. It doesn't make sense."

"Right. It doesn't make sense now, given the little we know about their relationship. If they've shared a lifetime of history, maybe she has secrets he's threatening to reveal."

"What kind of secrets?"

I shrug. "It could be anything. I've just come to warn you that if the cops are questioning Noah, it's a matter of hours until they question you more thoroughly."

"Then they'll question Wanda too."

"Pay lip service to questioning her, anyway. I sensed she and Detective Smythe knew each other. Though I'm not sure how well."

"Very well, I'd imagine, especially since she's running for mayor. They cross paths at meetings and so forth. They both grew up here, too."

"So if you, Noah, and Wanda didn't kill Mr. Pinkley, who's left?"

Brad paces the room. "Pinkley's lived in Florida for years—runs all kinds of crazy businesses. Maybe he got involved with the mob and it was an assassination."

I hadn't thought of that scenario. "Okay. But would the mob bother with a dancing-knife show? From what I've read, they just get in, make the hit, and get out fast."

Brad pours himself a drink from the bourbon bottle sitting on the stand near his bed.

"Bad habits die hard," he says, almost reading my thoughts. His eyes may be bloodshot, but his impish grin instantly wipes the wear and tear from his face.

I fight the delicious tingles welling up inside me. For a moment, I'm thirteen again, entranced by his picture on the cover of my aunt's *Food & Wine* magazine. He'd worn tight jeans, a white toque, and a smile.

There's so much I want to say. But I don't trust myself sitting here with him just ten feet from that bed. It takes all the willpower in my body to get to my feet and stand.

"Holly and I are taking the train back to Manhattan. There's nothing else to say but goodbye."

Still seated, Brad looks at me. "Do you really just want to say goodbye?" He pulls me down to his lap.

"Brad, I—"

He lowers his soft lips to mine. They brush against me like butterfly wings. It takes a moment to realize the rapid beating sensation I feel comes from my heart. This is the moment I've waited for—ever since I walked into his kitchen on LA's glamorous Restaurant Row over four years ago. And now, for the first time, Brad is kissing me. *Me.*

I force myself to rise. But Brad's holding me down. Still kissing me.

Only *kissing* isn't the right word. He nibbles my lips. I like the way his teeth gently bite. And while he nibbles, his hand explores the contours of my body, moving over my breasts and thighs. I eagerly kiss him back, sucking the sweetness from his lips. And biting a little myself.

Now his hand ventures to my inner thigh. I welcome it, but no.

It's too soon.

As much as I crave Brad, am I ready for something physical with him?

What I felt for Brad back when I was a busser in his restaurant might best be described as a schoolgirl crush. He's one of the most complex men I've ever met.

What would it be like to have an adult relationship with him? Or just an adult encounter? Beneath his quick charm, I've always sensed he's not an easy man. Gossip-magazine accounts of his torrid affairs with models and actresses confirm this.

The gentle circles of his fingers on my jean-covered thighs feel so good, but I force myself to wiggle out of his grasp.

"I came to say goodbye. Not this."

He flashes that sexy grin again. "Why not *this*?"

"Because." I smooth out my clothing and take a few steps backward. "Look, Brad, the time we shared during our picnic was magical. But I'm not ready for a fling."

"It doesn't have to be a fling."

I let that statement hang in the air before arching an eyebrow. "Brad Collins in a *relationship*?" Would he get into a relationship? *With me?* The thought makes me weak in the knees.

He says nothing, just smiles again.

"Okay. Let's be rational about this," I tell him. "If we were to go to the next step, it wouldn't begin here, in your bedroom. We'd have to get to know one another first."

"But we know one another."

"You *think* I know you because you're so famous. *But do you even know yourself?* If you did, you wouldn't have gone overboard punching that sous chef. You would have known when to stop."

Brad opens his mouth to speak, but in the end, he just shrugs. "Okay, Nina. Let's see what the future holds."

We look at one another for a long moment.

"Do you and Holly need a ride to the train station?"

Mr. Grant said he'd arranged a driver for us, but I want to spend as much time with Brad as possible. So I nod. "That would be great. Thanks."

CHAPTER 37

*A*s I carry my suitcase down the staircase, I take a last look at the portrait of Henrietta. She wears a serene expression.

Can she be resigned to letting me go? "Goodbye, Henrietta."

I take a last look at the Salem Heritage House, too. Mr. Pinkley certainly saw the potential here. In the right hands, this house could really be something.

Before I open the front door, I glance at one of the open boxes Moses has packed with Mr. Pinkley's items— silk shirts, linen slacks, and leather belts with impressive buckles. The other box holds more utilitarian items from his desk: various file folders, scissors, and strangely, an old-fashioned cassette tape resting on top.

I've seen a few other cassette tapes like that in my mother's junk box. And more recently, in Lillian's library office. Curious, I study the cryptic handwriting on the label: *Wanda Got Ya.*

When Lillian gave me the library tour, I saw the high school photo of Witch Wanda and Earnest Pinkley together. She said they had been good friends back in high school, maybe even secret lovers. Had Mr. Pinkley recorded a song for her? Or made some kind of mix tape?

But a cassette tape with the title *Wanda Got Ya* suggests other possibilities. I slip the cassette into my bag, feeling a tinge of guilt. But gut instinct suggests it may come in handy.

"Nina." The front door opens, and Holly pokes her head inside. "Brad's outside and ready for us. Let's go."

I join her in the brilliant sunshine, now that the morning's clouds have cleared away. Before us stands a classic black and white Cadillac, boasting a fresh paint job and a red leather interior. Brad, wearing a tight, white T-shirt and slim-fitting jeans, leans against it. He resembles a model on the cover of a wildly sexy romance novel.

"I didn't know you were into classic cars," I tell him.

He shakes his head. "I'm not. Pinkley had a garage full of them. One of my duties was to drive them around town and show them off. I might as well give this one a last spin."

Brad gallantly opens the back door for Holly and Jasper. Then he opens the front passenger door for me.

Even though the Caddie is decades old, its interior smells like new leather. When Brad starts the car, I look out the window at my last view of Salem. *Will I ever see it again?*

As we drive, I'm hyper aware of Brad sitting inches from me. The afternoon sun illuminates his aristocratic features.

When the Salem train station comes into view, I realize this may be the last time I'll see him. Who knows if he'll actually contact me, or if he's serious about trying some kind of relationship?

I try to think of something clever to say, but then I hear a siren. Flashing lights appear in the rearview mirror. "The police are pulling you over, Brad."

His lips press together, and his eyes narrow into slits of determination. The car speeds up. *Is he trying to make a run for it?*

But then the old car coughs, chokes, and abruptly dies a sputtering death. Now there's nothing Brad can do but pull over.

The police car slows and stops behind us. Brad's body tenses as he grasps his door handle, as if he's preparing to escape.

"No, Brad." I put my hand on his knee, as if my touch alone could stop him. *Why would he run? What does he have to hide?*

Two cops approach the driver's side window. "Brad Collins. Hands up. Step outside. You're under arrest for murder."

Shock washes over me. Unable to move, I can only watch as the police handcuff Brad. After searching him for weapons, they escort him to the rear seat of the police car.

Then they drive away.

"What just happened, Holly?" I turn toward my friend. "How can they arrest Brad?"

Holly shakes her head. "I had a feeling something like this might happen. We'd better grab our luggage and hightail it to the station or we'll miss the train."

I shake my head, resolve forming in my gut. "I'm not leaving Salem. Not until we sort this out."

 r. Grant appears startled to see us when we return to the Salem Heritage House.

"Ladies, what happened? I arranged for a driver, but—"

"Can we stay one more night?" I ask. "The police took Brad to the station. I need to sort this out."

He sighs. "I'd like to say yes, but it's not up to me. The Salem Preservation Committee is now in control of Ernest Pinkley's estate. They've sent instructions that the house be cleared."

The moving boxes I saw earlier have now been taped closed.

"We missed our train," Holly says.

"I'll check the schedule for the next one," Mr. Grant offers. "Please make yourselves comfortable until I get that information for you."

Holly nods. "That would be great."

When Mr. Grant leaves the room, I turn to Holly. "I'm going to see Detective Smythe. You'll be okay here alone?"

Before she can answer, I'm out the door and almost around the block.

The November wind smacks my face as I hasten toward the police station. When I arrive, I push open the heavy, gray doors. Inside, the scent of stale potato chips, dust, and sweat greets my nostrils.

"Hello. I'm Nina Brown," I tell the young man wearing a neatly pressed police officer's uniform at the counter. "I'd like to speak to Detective Smythe."

"Is he expecting you?"

"Yes," I lie.

"Take a seat, and I'll tell him you're here."

I choose the cleanest of the orange, prefabricated seats near the window. After brushing away potato chip crumbs, I sit down. The jarring sounds of ringing phones, file cabinets slamming, and intercom announcements keep me on edge.

What can I do for Brad Collins, really? Especially since I'm the only one who seems to care about him. He claims Wanda's his friend, *but where is she now?*

After a few minutes, Detective Smythe stands in front of me, stopping my wild train of thought.

"Ms. Brown. Come with me."

I follow him through the station. We pass a group of rough-looking men in the waiting area. Their hoots, hollers, and whistling assault my ears.

Finally, Detective Smythe leads me toward the private offices. I can't shake the jittery feeling of being watched by the overhead cameras above. He motions me inside his office, then shuts the door. I feel a little nervous being alone with him behind the closed door.

"Take a load off," he says.

I sit on the hard, beige plastic chair in front of his gray, government-regulation desk. The number of small, framed photos cluttering its surface surprises me. Most show him posing with cops in uniform. In a few photographs, he stands with men in suits, likely politicians.

But then I spot a picture of him with a woman I recognize immediately.

"Is that you with Witch Wanda?"

"Yep.

"Are you two friends?"

"I hope so. She's going to be our next mayor. What is it you've come to tell me?"

Brad mentioned that the two of them had an association. But it must be deeper than either of us thought if he has a picture of her on his office desk.

"Brad Collins is innocent. And I'd like to elaborate on what I saw last night."

"I already took your statement. Has your story changed?"

"Of course not. But now that the heat of the moment has passed, we have time to sort through the possibilities together."

"Ms. Brown, I'm a very busy man."

"Let's start with the report on those spiked brownies."

"What spiked brownies?"

"The brownies Brad ingested earlier last night as he prepared dinner. As the evening wore on, he appeared drugged. I noticed that right away. I told your police officer to take them in for analysis."

The detective reaches for a pen. "What was this police officer's name? I never received this request."

"He wrote it down as I stood before him. I assumed he'd take care of it."

Detective Smythe puts down his pen. "And the brownies are important for what reason?"

I take a deep breath. "As you and Wanda Williams

seem to be friends, you probably won't want to hear this. But she sent Brad spiked brownies yesterday. She was trying to drug him into a passive state so he wouldn't be savvy to her plan, or she hoped the brownies would make him bold enough to kill Mr. Pinkley."

"Why would Wanda want Mr. Pinkley dead?"

"I'm not sure. *Yet.* But Brad's convict status makes him a convenient scapegoat for the actual killer."

"I'm afraid you're too late," he says, rising. "Chef Collins is under arrest for murder in the first degree."

"On what evidence? You can't just make things up."

He shakes his head. "We have evidence all right. Brad Collins' chef's knife. Forensics found Ernest Pinkley's blood on it."

"But there must be a logical reason for that. It was taken from him. So was Wanda's athame and Noah's cutlass."

Detective Smythe stands, his gigantic presence towering above me. "I'd forget all about him, Ms. Brown. We're prepared to lock him up and throw away the key."

CHAPTER 39

Outside the police station, I consider my next move.
With her background in Las Vegas stage magic,
Wanda could easily have masterminded that illusion of a
knife dance. She had the opportunity to plant evidence
against Brad and deflect any blame from herself.

And if my hunch is right, she's working with Smythe to
make sure she'll never be found guilty of the crime.

But how can I prove it? And what was her motive?

Sure, she resented Mr. Pinkley for his plan to buy up,
build out, and modernize Salem for his own financial
benefit. But she didn't need to kill him to thwart his plan.
She could just sway fellow members of the preservation
committee to vote against him.

There *has* to be another reason.

Lillian said Wanda and Mr. Pinkley had been friends in
high school. Maybe even lovers. *With Wanda running to be
Salem's next mayor, could Mr. Pinkley be blackmailing her with
something from the past?*

Excited by this new idea, I hurry down the street.
Despite the cold weather, children clog the library's front

steps, reading books and chatting with friends. Other kids use the bottom steps to show off their skateboarding skills.

Zigzagging around them, I climb the stairs and enter the library's interior. After a moment, I spot Lillian sitting in a roped off area on the main floor. A circle of preschool-aged fans sit before her.

Walking closer, I'm touched by how intensely the children respond to Lillian's dramatic gestures and the intonations of her voice. When she closes the picture book, they clap their hands. Two of the kids give her a high-five before running off to their mothers.

"That must have been a great story."

"*The Cat in the Hat.* A classic." She rises and greets me with a hug. "But what are you doing here? I thought you were leaving Salem today."

A child shrieks somewhere behind us.

"I'll explain. But can we go someplace quieter?"

Once settled in Lillian's office, I tell her everything that's transpired since last night, including Brad's arrest. "I know Wanda may be your friend, but Brad is your friend, too. I need your help to clear his name."

"What makes you think Wanda is the culprit?" she asks.

"Wanda was pushing hard against development in her mayoral campaign. And Mr. Pinkley was all about expansion and renovating the Salem Heritage House. He could have threatened to expose some secret from her past if she didn't sway the preservation committee to allow his plans."

Lillian nods. "I can see him *making* the threat. But you're giving Wanda far too much credit. I'm part of the committee too, along with Blair's grandmother and some other well-respected local citizens. Wanda wouldn't have been able to sway *us*."

I'm silent for a moment. I've seen Blair's grandmother just that one time during the morning picnic with Brad. Yet I'd bet that if Pinkley wrote a big enough check, anything is possible.

"Wanda's mayoral campaign was at stake. You said she and Mr. Pinkley were good friends in high school. Good friends often share secrets. What if Mr. Pinkley threatened to expose a secret that would disqualify her from the office? And perhaps have her see jail time to boot. Could you see Wanda orchestrating his murder in that situation?"

"Hypothetically, yes. Within these library walls, many characters have been driven to murder for that very reason."

I take out my notebook and flip to the notes I took when I interviewed Lillian yesterday morning.

"Yesterday you told me Wanda started her career as a young witch telling fortunes on Essex Street. Then you mentioned something about voodoo. Black magic. And something else that I can't quite read. It looks like I wrote the word *German*, but I don't have any context around it."

"Ah, yes. The German. Wanda must have been in her last year of high school when he came to town."

"What was he doing here?"

"Seeing the sites. He'd been fascinated by witchcraft and wanted to see where it all happened. He was a young man, maybe in his early twenties."

"Tell me more about him."

Lillian's pale blue eyes mist over. She looks to her left as she recalls the foreigner. "Well, he was handsome. But more than handsome, he was what some people call a *gentleman*—at least he looked the part, with his tie and expensive suit. He swept Wanda off her feet."

"How did they meet?"

"At the trial, it was speculated they met at the Whale Head bar."

"Trial? What happened?"

"Well, they found the German dead. His body washed up on shore. Many were quick to point to Wanda as the killer, saying she'd worked her black magic on him. But in the end, his death was ruled a suicide, and the case was closed."

"Do you think Mr. Pinkley blackmailed her with that?"

"How could he? Assuming your notion of blackmail is even correct, this is *old news*—over twenty years old, and certainly no secret."

"Okay, but what if someone had genuine evidence that she *used* black magic to drive the German to his death? And that person threatened to reveal this evidence unless she did what he requested. No one, even in Salem, would vote for a witch using black magic."

"True. Provided there was genuine evidence."

"This might be a way to find out." I take the cassette tape from the Salem Heritage House out of my bag. "I noticed your cassette player during our conversation yesterday. May I use it to play this tape?"

"Of course." She spins around and puts the cassette player on the desk. Then she pops out the tape inside. "Old school, I know, but they're not making my favorite meditation music in other formats. Where's that cassette of yours from?"

"Moses packed a box of Mr. Pinkley's personal items. I found it odd for a man as wealthy and tech-savvy as Mr. Pinkley to have such old media. Then I caught sight of the title. *Wanda Got Ya*."

"Well, let's hear it, then."

The cassette tape is not in great condition, yet as we listen, Mr. Pinkley's voice is audible. It sounds like he's trying to calm a very hysterical Wanda. But age has warped the fragile material of the audiotape. Mr. Pinkley's voice becomes distorted, and the tape physically breaks.

"I gave it my best shot." I take a deep breath. "Back in New York, I'll try to see if we can salvage this tape."

"Why not give it to Detective Smythe? I'm sure the police department has the technology for this kind of thing."

"Oh no. I wouldn't be surprised if Detective Smythe is in cahoots with Witch Wanda."

"You think so?" she asks, surprised. After a moment, she nods. "Come to think of it, I have noticed they appear friendly to one another at civic meetings."

I stand. "Brad idolizes you, Lillian. He wanted to co-write that Early American cookbook with you. If you can think of anything that might help his defense, please call me."

After handing her my business card, and we hug each other tightly before I leave.

Holly jumps to her feet as soon as I enter the Salem Heritage House. Hands on hips, she looks me up and down. "Where were you all this time? I was worried sick. Jasper, too."

He yips to underscore her point.

"After the police station, I visited Lillian at the library. I'm going to do a final check of our room before we leave."

"Better make it snappy. We could face lots of traffic with everyone traveling home after the Halloween weekend. I'm taking Jasper to the kitchen to see if there's anything for him to eat."

Once upstairs in our suite, I look up at Henrietta's portrait. Today she looks like she's trying to hide a big secret. The way she meets my gaze is like looking at my image in the mirror. As if I'm *looking at myself.* Is Henrietta still inside me? Moses said I had the power to expel her, but he didn't tell me how to do it.

Pyewacket slithers in through the slightly open window. I haven't seen her since she and Lillian played together before the séance. She meows and jumps on to the bed, looking up at me.

"I'll miss you, Pyewacket." Unable to resist the look in her jewel-toned eyes, I stroke the silky black fur behind her ears.

Pyewacket raises her paw to touch my scar. Her touch has the warmth of my father's last kiss before that horrific car accident ripped him from my life. Then, her paw yanks the gold locket from my throat.

"Pyewacket!"

She scampers away with the necklace between her teeth. Pyewacket dives beneath Henrietta's fancy white dresser and flips up the edge of the Persian carpet. Mr. Grant must have positioned it there to hide the gaping hole I can now see in the two-hundred-year-old floorboards.

I race to grab her, but Pyewacket disappears into the crawlspace. Using the flashlight on my phone, I illuminate what appears to be a narrow tunnel built as a vertical secret passage. It includes a series of metal toe and handholds leading dozens of feet down to the basement.

Looking down at its fathomless depths, my stomach turns somersaults, and my heart beats wildly. Every instinct in my body demands that I turn away. *But how can I turn away when that locket is my cherished connection with my father?*

I must have it back.

Rather than lose my most prized possession, I fight my racing heart and shortness of breath as I shove the dresser aside. Then, inch by inch, I lower myself down through the shaft.

When my feet finally touch firm ground, I find myself in a cellar. Resting on the dirt floor are dozens of boarded-up crates, some old furniture too. Everything is caked with centuries of dust. Pyewacket is nowhere to be seen.

I use my phone again for illumination. The beam of light exposes cobwebs and containers, but no cat. Eventually, a soft meow exposes Pyewacket's position on a cobweb-covered crate to my right. My gold necklace sparkles between her teeth in the beam of my flashlight.

"It's okay, Pyewacket," I say, reaching out for it. "The game is over. This necklace is very important, so please give it back."

But Pyewacket leaps away, this time jumping to a coffin-shaped crate caked in dust and soot. She looks at me, as if to make sure I'm following. Then, like a model showing a product on a shopping network show, she glides her paw over the metal bracket that's locking the oddly shaped crate together. A not-so-subtle feline request to open it.

Oh, man. What can be in that long, human-sized crate? A dead body? *Henrietta's body?*

No. Noah said they buried both Henrietta and Captain Hawkins at Charter Street Cemetery. *Whose body can this be?*

My first instinct is to call Mr. Grant. But then I'd risk Pyewacket running away with my locket and leaving it somewhere I could never find again. I force myself to reach out and unfasten the latch of the coffin-like crate.

At least if there's a body inside, it's already dead.

Hopefully. Who knows if vampires lurk in the Salem Heritage House, too?

With Pyewacket still on top of the dusty crate, I open the brackets. "I'm opening it. Is that what you wanted?"

The cat jumps off the box and settles a comfortable distance from me. She seems intent on not giving me back my locket until I do her bidding.

The crate creaks open with an agonizing groan and a cloud of dust. Peering inside, I'm relieved not to see any flesh or bones. The box is lined in red velvet, but the fabric's now dull and eaten away, covered with soot.

Inside rests a leather-bound book. A journal.

On the front are the words *Henrietta's Diary*.

"Mr. Grant?" I fly up the staircase, two steps at a time. In my right hand, I hold both my locket and Henrietta's diary. The leather feels soft and almost moldy, but from the few pages I've skimmed, Henrietta's pen strokes are clear and easy to read. "Mr. Grant."

Pyewacket follows, holding her head high.

I find him in Captain Hawkins' office, with a box of dusty old books near his feet.

Though I'm bursting to blurt out the news, I compose myself first. "What are you doing? Boxing up Captain Hawkins' books?"

"Yes. At the request of the preservation committee. They're considering auctioning them off."

"That's a shame. I've rarely seen such a magnificent private library. Mr. Pinkley didn't have any relatives? Not even any cousins?"

He shakes his head. "None. His parents died young, and they had no siblings. Now what can I help you with, Ms. Brown?" He flashes his dazzling smile.

"I found it." I grin, unable to contain my excitement any longer. I show him the journal. "Henrietta's diary. I found it in the basement."

Mr. Grant removes his smart-looking glasses and edges closer. "Indeed. How do you know it's hers?"

"Her name is embossed in gold right on the cover, and the last entry is from the year Captain Hawkins was murdered."

"Well, now, what does it say?" Mr. Grant emits that dapper movie star laugh of his. "Does she reveal the location of the treasure everyone's been trying to find all these years?"

"I haven't gotten that far. But it turns out Henrietta had a secret baby. Well, she tried to keep it a secret. She wrote that one night she seduced Captain Hawkins. By the time she discovered she was pregnant, he was off to sea. She gave the boy up for adoption. Then she married and had another son by her legal husband, the man who hired thugs to kill Captain Hawkins. *His* son must be Pinkley's ancestor."

"And what of the first son?" Mr. Grant asks.

"Alive at the time of her writing. I bet Lillian will help me track what became of him. If his descendants are alive today, she'll find them."

"May I see the diary?"

I hand it over. As Mr. Grant reads, my locket burns hot around my neck, nearly scorching me. I shift my weight from one foot to the other. He's certainly taking his time looking through the pages. "Excuse me, Mr. Grant. But I need to bring it over to Lillian at the library as soon as possible. May I have it back now, please?"

"Of course. But before you go, I want to show you something I found that may exonerate your friend Brad."

"What is it?"

"Wanda's athame. She must have dropped it after killing Pinkley."

"So you agree that she killed him?"

"Is there any doubt? Wanda killed Pinkley, then dropped her athame in the secret passageway leading to the roof walk as she made her escape. She re-entered the house, and when the lights went back on, she pretended she'd been there all along. Come. Let me show you her route."

Mr. Grant leads me toward the sliding glass door to the rectangular roof walk. Even safely behind the glass, my head spins, anticipating the sheer drop.

He slides the door open, takes my hand, and pulls me out.

Just minutes ago, when my locket was at risk, I fought my acrophobia to descend through a steep, narrow space.

But now I stand frozen.

"I love this roof walk. Some call it a widow's walk, of course—a classic piece of New England architecture. Look, you can see the Atlantic Ocean through the iron railing."

"Beautiful." Feeling unsteady, I sway a little on my feet.

"Behold, Wanda's athame. Look closely, and you can still see Pinkley's blood."

Mr. Grant yanks me toward the low iron gate. Near it lies Wanda's black witching knife, with dull, rusty red blood at its tip.

"I'm going inside." But when I turn, Mr. Grant snaps me back.

"No. You're going out. Or rather, down. Down to the sidewalk. *Splat.* I'm sure with your fear of heights that's not your favorite way to die, but alas, it's the only option available."

"Why would you kill me? Unless—" I gasp. "Did you kill Mr. Pinkley?"

"I did, indeed."

"But why?"

"I would have let the fool live. We had a good business going together. I could manage him. But he has a sharp eye, that Pinkley. He caught some *inconsistencies*, shall we call them, in our accounting books. He accused me of pilferage."

"But you could have just left the Salem Heritage House. You didn't have to kill him."

He scoffs. "Of course, I did. With Pinkley dead, I can continue my work without obstruction. I'll sweet-talk the preservation committee into letting me manage the Salem Heritage House in a *responsible* way, without unnecessary renovations. At the same time, I'll remain here at the hotel so I can continue my search for Pinkley's treasure. With that diary, you're saving me a lot of trouble."

"Let me go. One murder is bad enough. But when they find you've killed me too, you'll hang."

"You underestimate my skill. I'm a magician—ten years a star at London's Shaftsbury theater. *I make illusions real*. That was my tagline, by the way."

"You were the one who suggested Wanda convince Mr. Pinkley to hire an ex-con as the hotel chef. So you could make Brad a fall guy for your murder plot."

Mr. Grant shakes his head. "Wanda was behind that, for all the right reasons. But I soon realized Brad *would* be the ideal person to take the blame for Pinkley's murder. Of course, I had to set things up so Wanda could be an alternate choice if the charges against Brad didn't stick."

"It won't take the police long to realize you killed me."

"Not with this suicide note."

My blood runs cold as Mr. Grant takes a neatly folded

paper from his pocket. "You were distraught, Nina—upset that the love of your life would rot behind bars. There was no reason for you to live."

"The cops would never trust a typed suicide note."

"It has your signature on it." Mr. Grant flashes it at me before he folds it back into his pocket.

"How did you get my signature?"

"Remember, I asked you to sign in at the register when you first arrived? I had a carbon under that. Classic magician's trick."

"You knew you were going to kill me as soon as I arrived? *Before* I arrived? When I first contacted you about advertising with my magazine?"

"Not quite that far in advance, no. And I had no intention of killing you at all. But you've overstayed your welcome, dear Nina. And we hoteliers can't have that now, can we?"

Panic rises within me. *Mr. Grant is crazy.* A cool, meticulous killer.

"Well, Nina, I would like to say it was nice knowing you. You impressed me the moment our negotiations began. It took guts for a secretary at a fancy magazine to cold call me like that and pitch your advertising plan. Maybe you can put that talent to better use in your next life."

Reaching into his pocket, Mr. Grant removes a small silver revolver. He aims it at me. "Now keep walking backward. In exactly nine seconds, you'll reach that low iron gate. Feel free to flip yourself over. Or allow me the pleasure of tossing you overboard."

I shake my head. "Not logical. No one will believe a woman with acrophobia would toss herself from a great height. You'll have to shoot me first. How will you explain that?"

"The gun is just to scare you. It would barely take the force of my little finger to push you over the ledge."

At that moment, a flash of black flies through the air. *Pyewacket.*

She lands on top of Mr. Grant's head and rakes her claws across the hotel manager's cheek. Blood spurts through the air. When he drops his gun to tear the cat from his face, I grab it. I know all I need to do is pull the trigger. But I stand there in shock.

"Holy guacamole." Holly appears beside me and quickly takes stock of the situation. She grabs my arm and pulls me back to the staircase while Mr. Grant continues fighting off Pyewacket. "Let's move it."

As we race down the stairs, I'm too distraught to register the expression on Henrietta's face in her portrait.

Once we're out the front door, Holly calls 911 and tells the operator we have an emergency. Then she turns to me, breathless. "What the heck happened?"

"Mr. Grant was trying to kill me." Holly's eyes grow wide as I tell her everything he said. "He's a sharp talker," I conclude, shaking my head as we hear police sirens in the distance. "What if he fast-talks his way out of everything? What if the cops don't believe he killed Mr. Pinkley? Then Brad will never get out of jail."

Holly takes my hand. "Let's cross that bridge when we come to it."

CHAPTER 42

*L*ater that evening, Flying Saucer Pizza buzzes with activity. For the last 24 hours, the murder of Ernest Pinkley and the recent capture of the prime suspect Theodore Grant have been the key subject on everyone's lips.

All eyes follow our small group as the hostess leads us to our table. Most whisper as we pass. As soon as we're seated, Holly asks for a booster seat for Jasper.

"Well, ladies," Noah says. "I must ask if you're surprised that Mr. Grant turns out to be the prime suspect. It's a complete surprise to me."

"Really?" I ask. "Then who did you think killed Mr. Pinkley?"

Noah hesitates. "As a loyal son of Salem, I'd like to think it was the work of Captain Hawkins himself."

"You can't mean that," I say. "Hollywood shenanigans aside, there's not much a translucent ghost can do to kill a living person. They don't have enough force to pull the trigger on a gun. They're not solid enough to hold a knife."

"But they can *scare* people to death," says Holly, helping

The Jasp settle into his bright red plastic booster chair when it arrives.

"True enough," says Noah. "I didn't know Brad all that well, but I felt he was being framed. Don't forget, I was considered a suspect, too."

I take a deep breath. "I'm just glad it's over."

The Jasp, sitting upright with his paws on the table, yips sharply when the door opens. I look up, surprised to see Blair Blanning. Today she's dressed in a psychedelic pink, black, and white 1960s shift with a wide white collar and white go-go boots. She heads directly toward our table.

"Noah, ladies, hi," she says. "May I take a seat?"

Before any of us can give our consent, she pulls out a chair and grabs my menu.

"To what do we owe this pleasure, Blair?" Noah says.

"I heard Mr. Grant was arrested. I'm hoping you'll fill me in on the details."

"You can read it in the *Salem News* tomorrow morning," I say coldly.

"Nina's just being modest. She and Lillian figured it all out at the library, as soon as the cops took Mr. Grant to jail," says Holly.

"Figured out what?" Blair asks, smiling.

"Theodore Grant was a famous illusionist in London years ago," I say. "He had an act involving dancing knives. Lillian found footage in the library's archive. He used that same stunt the night of the séance. His knowledge of the secret passageways in the Salem Heritage House allowed him to move freely, kill Mr. Pinkley, and then make it seem like Brad was the culprit."

"But why would Theodore Grant want to kill Mr. Pinkley?"

"Mr. Grant admitted that he'd been extorting money from Mr. Pinkley's bank account, and Mr. Pinkley recently found out. Then he tried to force me to jump off the widow's walk."

"I can believe Grant killing Pinkley," says Blair. "But why would he bother killing you?"

"I'd just found Henrietta's diary in the basement. He wanted it for himself, so he could find the treasure. Is there anything else you'd like to know? In case you're interested, Lillian's turned the diary over to the Salem Preservation Committee for safekeeping. So I'd think twice before you *twitch your nose* to magically acquire it."

When the server comes to take our order, he asks Blair what she'd like first.

"I'm not staying," she says, putting down her menu. "In fact, I'm going to borrow Nina for a moment. I'll bring her right back. I promise."

Curious about what she might want to tell me, I follow Blair outside the restaurant.

"I owe you a big apology," she says.

"For what?"

"Long story." She leads me to a small white bench a few feet from the restaurant. "Let me start by telling you I never meant you any harm."

"Any harm? What do you mean?"

"It's like this. I've been fascinated by Henrietta since I was a little kid. One day, Lillian sent us children on a scavenger hunt. We weren't permitted to enter the Salem Heritage House, but I found a way inside through a crawlspace in the basement. I was searching for her diary but found a bunch of loose pages instead. It took me years to realize those pages contained a set of instructions and spells to bring her back to life."

"Why are you telling me this now?"

"Because Henrietta identified you as the new vessel for her incarnation."

For a moment, I'm unable to speak. "You'd dare perform a spell to enable a deceased human being to live in *my body*?"

"Yes—no. I mean, if it's any comfort, I was hoping Henrietta would choose *my body*. My idea was that once Henrietta was inside of me, we'd figure out where Captain Hawkins hid his treasure. Then we'd use the money to travel the world and live large. Salem is unbelievably boring, if you haven't noticed."

"Continue, please."

"As soon as you arrived at the Salem Heritage House, Henrietta decided she wanted your body. Probably because you looked so much alike. She charged me with making the transformation."

"Captain Hawkins used that word with me during the séance. Do you think he was influencing Henrietta?"

"Maybe," Blair says. "They were lovers, even though she was his ward. She had his child, her first son, though she put him up for adoption. But the important thing I'm trying to tell you is that when you go back to New York, you won't be going alone."

"Of course not. I'll be going back with Holly and Jasper."

"And Henrietta."

"What?"

"Before the séance, I saw my opportunity to make the transformation Henrietta demanded in those pages I'd found as a child. I had everything prepared. And according to the spell Henrietta left, I summoned you to arrive at exactly the right time. She was to permeate your soul. But then that darn cat went wild, and all hell broke loose."

I think back to the night of the séance, just twenty-four hours ago, though it seems much longer. "I don't remember anything like that."

"That's because I put a 'forget' spell on you. You need to know that I *started* the spell, but the transformation is not complete."

"What's that supposed to mean?"

Blair looks at me like I'm the dullest tool in the shed. "That Henrietta's spirit has settled inside you, but the transformation ritual was interrupted before she could fully overtake your body."

Under ordinary circumstances, I'd think Blair was certifiably mad. But this has been no ordinary weekend. "What do you hope to accomplish by speaking with me tonight?"

"I found a way to reverse the spell," she says. "Or at least to use the principle of transference to bring her into my body. Henrietta's explicitly given her permission for me to do so, since she's discovered your life is not as exciting as she initially thought."

I'm not sure whether to feel relieved or insulted. "Henrietta thinks my life is boring?"

"I don't want to put words in her mouth. But when she first met you, she liked your looks and that you live in Manhattan."

"And now that she knows me?"

Blair presses her lips together. "Let's just say she's come to favor me as her preferred partner. She's given me the okay to book travel to the South of France next summer. Of course, we'll be going to a language school. At least that's what I'll tell my grandmother."

"And the money to finance your new jet-setting lifestyle?"

"That will all come in due course."

"What about Pyewacket? She's your familiar now, if what you told me is true."

"She'll come with us. Any other questions?"

"Just one. What is Moses' involvement in all this?"

Blair shrugs. "Henrietta likes him well enough. He practically raised her after her parents died at sea."

"Was he the one who taught her the dark arts?"

Blair's eyes flash as she looks up at me. "How did you know?"

"I found a book about his tribe in Jharkhand in Captain Hawkins' study. His family were powerful witches. When the islanders turned against them, Captain Hawkins helped him escape with the gold. That's why Moses has been so loyal all these years. And speaking of years, is he the fifth generation Moses B. Anthony to guard the house, or the sixth?"

"Have you considered that they're all one and the same?" Blair asks. "Same story with Pyewacket. Man, you really are new to the world of magic, aren't you?"

"And the appearance of Captain Hawkins during the séance? Mr. Grant was a highly skilled illusionist; I'll give him that much. He really made Captain Hawkins' ghost seem real."

Blair frowns at me, then slowly shakes her head. "What makes you think his ghost *wasn't* real?"

Interesting. In Blair's world, loyal caretakers live for centuries and Salem sea captains never truly die.

"Okay. Let's play that out. Captain Hawkins revealed himself to me when I first arrived at the Salem train station. Why do you think his ghost manifested *this weekend?*"

"It must tie in with the anniversary of his murder and the transference of the Salem Heritage House to his oldest living heir," Blair says. "We all assumed that heir to be Mr. Pinkley."

"But during the séance, he confronted Mr. Pinkley and told him he would die. So clearly, Mr. Pinkley *wasn't* the favored heir to take ownership of the Salem Heritage House and its hidden treasure. Maybe the reason he manifested was to ensure that his house and fortune were given to his true heir, the illegitimate child he sired with Henrietta—*whoever that is*."

Blair looks at her watch. "It's getting late. Shall we start the ceremony?

"Don't you need privacy? Candles? Blood? An offering?"

"Not for a *reversal spell*," she says, rolling her eyes. "I just need you to keep quiet while I recite the incantation."

I close my eyes as Blair quietly whispers the spell. It's a long one, spoken in a strange language with a lively cadence. Suddenly, with no warning, I feel something large and dense eject from my body. The effort of expelling it leaves me breathless.

Blair stops her chanting. "Well, that's over," she says, rising.

"Wait. Are you saying Henrietta's left my body?"

"You felt it, didn't you?"

"Yes. But is she gone for good?"

"It's Henrietta's choice. Only time will tell."

*O*ne Year Later

"Everyone, may I have your attention, please?" Brad speaks from the front of the brand-new Pilgrims' Harvest restaurant, located inside the swank, newly redesigned Salem Heritage House. Rico's positioned himself on Brad's shoulder, looking down his beak at the crowd.

"I'd like you all to join me in singing 'Happy Birthday' to a very special VIP."

The lights dim. Illuminated by a spotlight overhead, Brad sings the happy birthday song as he carries a delicious-looking cake to our large table.

He places it before Jasper, sleek in a doggy tuxedo. The Jasp happily yips along with the tune, all the while flashing an adoring doggy smile to Holly and me.

"Happy birthday, mate," squawks Rico in that old-man croak of his. "Happy birthday, mate."

Guests applaud as we help our pampered pooch blow out the candles.

But when Barry Manilow's song "Copacabana" comes

on the loudspeaker, Rico leaps from Brad's shoulder to the table. The spotlight follows as he bobs his head and kicks his feet to match the song's catchy rhythm.

Brad faces Rico in a dance-off, shimmying his shoulders and shaking his booty. Guests leap to their feet and crowd our table to catch the action, camera phones in hand.

Jasper drops his head, covering his eyes and ears with his paws.

"The nerve of that bird," says Holly, shaking her head. "And on The Jasp's birthday too!"

When the song ends, applause for Rico's dance mixes with shrieks, whistles, and birdcalls.

Brad leans down to kiss my cheek and whispers, "you look fantastic." Then he winks and heads back to the kitchen.

"He's a sight for sore eyes," Holly says, admiring Brad's broad shoulders, sun-tousled blond hair, and cute, jeans-covered derriere as he walks away. "Is it my imagination, or has he become even hotter since the last time we saw him?"

I shrug. "That's what freedom can do for a man. Now that he's running his own restaurant, he's on top of the world," I say, taking a sip of Champagne.

"Do you regret not making a go of your relationship with him?" Holly asks. "He *wanted* you. And it looks like he still does, even now that he's New England's latest ground-breaking celebrity chef."

"*Wants* is the key word, Holly. Brad wants many things. He gets them, too. I just didn't want to be part of his collection. Besides, I'm not sure Rico will allow a third party in their relationship."

We both laugh, and I turn to face Noah on my left. "I must congratulate you on what you've done with this place.

Mr. Pinkley may have dreamed of attracting affluent, adoring guests to his hotel, but you really did it."

"With a little help from my friends." Noah smiles at me and Holly, and then at Lillian, sitting across from us. "I'm not sure how I could have found my family connection to Captain Hawkins without Lillian's help."

"Tell us, Noah, how does it feel to be rich, rich, rich?" Holly pops one of Brad's now-famous Early American cookies into her mouth.

"Rich?" Noah asks, seeming slightly uncomfortable in his black designer suit. He laughs. "All the improvements you see in the Salem Heritage House result from a *giant* redevelopment loan from the city. And that's thanks to Mayor Witch Wanda. I haven't found Captain Hawkins' treasure yet."

"I bet Moses B. Anthony knows where that treasure's hidden," says Holly, looking over at Moses as he directs the servers serving cake to all the guests. "How's he working out as your chief of staff, Noah? Is he freaking out now that he must deal with live guests instead of ghosts?"

"Moses is doing okay. I get the sense he's just happy to continue living and working in the Salem Heritage House. He's a good man."

"Lillian, have you found any clues about the treasure in Henrietta's diary?" I ask. "Noah might need that fortune to build this place out."

"Treasure? Who needs a treasure," says Noah's mother, a mostly silent, tiny lady sitting by his side. "My boy has everything he needs." She taps Holly affectionately on the shoulder. "Except *one thing.* When are you going to make an honest woman of Holly Broad, son? This girl's a winner."

Holly and Noah share a secret smile, with Noah gesturing for Holly to respond.

"Thanks, Mrs. Samuels. That's sweet. But we live in

two different cities. We tried the long- distance thing, but it didn't work out. We love being friends, though." Noah squeezes Holly's hand. Jasper puts his paw on top of their joined hands and yips his pleasure at seeing them together.

As the evening ends, Brad and I walk over to tonight's human VIP, my boss Ruth Ross, to bid her goodbye. Holly and Noah join us.

"How did you enjoy your dinner, Ms. Ross?" Brad asks.

Everyone at her table holds their breath in anticipation of the famously fussy editor's response.

"I'm impressed," says Ruth after a brief pause. "I must admit, when Nina pitched the idea of a luxury hotel in Salem a year ago, I had my doubts. Then, when she repackaged the pitch as The New Salem, I nearly gave up on the idea—especially since the article promised to focus on an ex-con celebrity chef making his comeback. But this night is proof positive that Salem has achieved culinary fame."

"Thank you," says Brad.

"I find your Early American cuisine to be what everyone wants to eat. 'Nourishment from the earth' is the catchphrase of today—healthy food everyone wants to eat and enjoy. We received more recipe requests from your issue than ever before."

Holly leans toward me to whisper in my ear. "That magazine cover showing Brad in tight jeans lying in a cabbage patch might have had something to do with it."

I elbow her.

Ruth turns to Noah. "And what you've done with this historic inn is amazing. One of my friends is the editor of *Architectural Digest*. I bet he'd be interested in featuring the Salem Heritage House for an upcoming story."

As an overjoyed Noah and Ruth discuss the details,

Blair Blanning catches my eye. It's the first I've seen or heard of her for almost a year.

She sits with two other girls, identically dressed in the navy jackets and plaid skirts of a prep school.

Or more likely, a magical academy.

Then I remember Noah telling me that as the first witch mayor of Salem, Wanda set up a foundation for civic-minded witches in training. Within this city-sponsored program, young people can learn the magical arts under the guidance of an *ethical* witch.

I glance at my watch. In less than thirty minutes, Holly and I will take a private car back to Manhattan, courtesy of *Travel! Food! Wine!* magazine.

Time is short.

I gravitate toward Henrietta's portrait near the stairwell. In it, she looks as she always has — young, beautiful, with a hint of mystery. But missing from my initial visit is that vivid trompe l'oeil expression in her eyes.

Something soft and furry brushes against my ankles.

"Pyewacket!" I scoop up the tiny feline, holding her before me so our eyes meet. She looks alert, healthy, and even happy, from what I can decipher of a cat's emotions. "I've missed you!" I nuzzle my head against her sleek body, then put her down.

I'm about to turn and leave when I detect a subtle movement in Henrietta's gaze. Then her lips curve into a smile.

I haven't finished with you yet.

WHERE WILL NINA TRAVEL NEXT, now that she's a rising star at the magazine? And of course Holly and Jasper will insist on tagging along!

Claim your copy of Spooked in Switzerland to follow their madcap adventures. *Love the magic of Provence, France?* Have fun sharing the experience of Nina, Holly, and Jasper as they solve a mystery in the first book of the series, Poisoned in Provence.

~

Laughed a lot reading Jasper's crazy antics? I sure had fun writing them!

Please help your fellow readers discover Jasper and the gang with a simple one or two sentence review for Silenced in Salem on the site from which you purchased the book, Goodreads, or your own blog. You are most welcome to email me the link or just say "hi" 🖐 at Cat@ CatGreenAuthor.com

~

Get fun "bonus content" when you join the VIP Catster community. You get a free eBook too, a story about Nina and Holly when they were in high school called About Last Night.

~

www.ingramcontent.com/pod-product-compliance
Lightning Source LLC
Chambersburg PA
CBHW020758190726
48285CB00006B/2091